DARKWATER HOUSE

SAMUEL KING

Darkwater House
ISBN # 978-1-83943-919-3
©Copyright Samuel King 2020
Cover Art by Louisa Maggio ©Copyright September 2020
Interior text design by Claire Siemaszkiewicz
Pride Publishing

DARKWATER HOUSE

Chapter One

When Toby first opened his eyes, he couldn't remember where he was. That wasn't unusual. It was Saturday morning, which meant the previous night had been the start of the weekend. For Toby, that generally involved downing as much alcohol as possible in the Black Swan pub — an old-school gay bar, where most of the clientele were thirty years older than Toby, but where he still met the odd cute guy. He lay staring at a blank cream-colored wall. It wasn't *his* bedroom wall. His bedroom wall was blue. So, he was in someone else's bed. Again, that wasn't unusual.

Being careful not to move and disturb whoever was lying next to him until he had remembered who they were, Toby began to piece together the evening as best he could. He'd drunk at least a bottle of wine in his flat before heading out on his own. He didn't have any close friends in London anymore, no one to make plans with on a Friday night. He'd upset them all at one point or another over the past two years. Toby was the first to admit that he'd become a bit of a dick since breaking up with Joe. Joe had been his last steady relationship. When Joe dumped him, Toby had felt like his life had been obliterated. He'd started drinking heavily, and when he drank heavily in company, he often got loud and insulting. One by one, his friends had begun to avoid him, until they weren't his friends anymore.

Along with the drinking had come the casual sex and the waking up in strange beds, with little or no memory of how he had got there.

After finishing the bottle of wine at home — a poky one-bedroom flat in Islington — he'd headed to the Black Swan, a ten-minute walk away. He'd ordered another bottle of wine and sat at a table in a corner at the back of the bar. It had been relatively quiet when he'd arrived, he recalled, because it was only around five-thirty in the evening. He'd started early.

The person lying next to Toby stirred and moaned. Toby had his back to him so was still in the dark as to his identity.

He had a brief flashback of a handsome guy in his thirties asking if the seat next to him was taken. A name popped into his head…Doug. *Is it Doug's bed I'm in?* A hairy, muscular arm wrapped itself around Toby's chest and Doug — or whoever it was — began to nuzzle the back of his neck. Now a hard cock was pressing against his arse.

I really hope this is Doug. Doug was hot.

He couldn't put it off any longer. He was going to have to turn around and face the stranger. He'd pretend to remember everything about their meeting, maybe have morning sex with them, if they were attractive. If it was Doug, morning sex would be a definite, unless his memory of Doug was a fake one.

Maybe he was seeing Doug through a hangover haze. Perhaps Doug wasn't as hot as he thought.

One, two, three...

Toby rolled over to face his lover of the previous night.

"Joe!"

His ex-boyfriend of two years ago grinned at him. He had gained a little weight and his hair was longer, but there was no doubt that the man lying next to him was Joe—the man who had destroyed his life.

"Who were you expecting?" asked Joe, kissing Toby on the mouth.

Toby floundered for an answer. How could he have forgotten pulling his ex? When had Joe arrived at the Black Swan?

Joe squinted at him. He had the most beautiful pale-blue eyes.

"You actually don't remember, do you?" he asked.

"Of course I do," said Toby, racking his brain for a fragment of memory that would help him bluff his way through the next few seconds.

"You came into the Black Swan and..."

"Wrong," said Joe, sitting up. The bedcovers fell, revealing his broad, hairy chest and a slight beer belly. Joe was tall and stocky enough to carry it off, though. A tantalizing tuft of pubic hair poked above the edge of the quilt.

"Shit," said Toby. "Where then?"

"I found you outside my flat," said Joe. "I didn't realize you even knew where I lived now."

Toby knew where Joe lived all right. He'd met one of his friends a few months before and managed to get the information without making it obvious he was grilling them. But how had he ended up here? Joe's new place was a half-hour drive from Islington, in Wimbledon, South London.

I must have taken a taxi.

"So, you found me outside and brought me in for a fuck?" asked Toby.

"Well, yeah," said Joe, running a hand through his blond hair. "I was drunk and horny too, and you were obviously here for sex."

"Wow," said Toby, "you always did make me feel special."

Joe laughed and threw back the quilt, revealing his now-semi-hard cock. Toby remembered that cock well — the solid feel of it in his hand, the taste of it. Had he sucked it last night? *How can I not remember?*

"It's been two years, Toby. I thought it would be okay to just have a bit of fun. I didn't realize you were so pissed that you wouldn't remember a thing. You didn't seem that drunk. You weren't even being obnoxious."

"Oh, fuck off," snapped Toby, climbing from the bed and searching the room for his clothes.

"They're in the hallway," said Joe, also standing, tugging on his balls and walking groggily to the adjoining bathroom.

Toby smelled of sex and stale alcohol. He wished he could shower before he left, but he also wanted to get away from this situation as soon as possible. If he didn't leave now, if he stayed for breakfast, he'd start to convince himself that something could happen between them again.

Joe poked his head around the bathroom door.

"I hate to be rude," he said, "but Mike, my boyfriend, is due home in about three hours and I want to get the bed changed and get rid of any other evidence. We have an open relationship, but I don't want to rub his nose in it."

If he'd needed any other excuse to make a quick escape, that was it.

Toby pulled open the bedroom door and stumbled into the narrow hallway, picking up items of clothing as he went. He found a second bathroom, had a brief wash and dressed. He stared at himself in the small mirror above the sink. He was barely recognizable. His once-chiseled face was puffy and blotchy, his eyes bloodshot, and his lips and teeth were stained with red wine. It was hard to see why Joe had been tempted. He could only imagine what he must have looked like in his drunken state the night before. Joe had obviously been equally inebriated to have even considered sleeping with Toby again after two years of avoiding him. Maybe things with the new boyfriend weren't as rosy as Joe wanted him to think.

Toby scrubbed at his stained lips with a flannel and did his best to clean his teeth with a finger and a dollop of toothpaste. He still looked a wreck, but it would have to do. He slipped out of the front door without saying goodbye.

There was a middle-aged woman standing on the doorstep of the house next door, smoking a cigarette. She was wearing a pink fleece dressing gown and was visibly shivering. As Toby stepped onto the front path, she cast a look in his direction. She gave an exaggerated puff on her cigarette as she looked him up and down. She acted as if she knew exactly what the situation was—maybe she even knew Joe's boyfriend. Toby focused on the road ahead, too fragile to deal with this stranger's disapproval.

It was cold and the street was deserted. He glanced at his watch. It was six thirty-five a.m. He stood, trying to decide which way might lead to a tube station. He considered asking Joe's neighbor, but when he glanced back, she was slipping into her house, throwing the cigarette butt onto the path behind her. After brief consideration, based on no knowledge of the area, he opted to turn left.

My life has got to change.

* * * *

"Excuse me."

For the second time that morning, Toby awoke not knowing where he was. On this occasion, the disorientation only lasted for a few seconds. He was on a tube train. The clatter of metal on metal hurt his head. It had taken him half an hour to find a station after leaving Joe's place. As soon as he'd sat down, he had started to drift off. He'd been dreaming about Joe, creating a more idyllic version of their reunion, where they were both sober and falling into each other's arms rather than staggering to Joe's bedroom, Joe too pissed to care that he might be opening up a romantic can of worms.

"Excuse me," came the voice again — a well-spoken male voice.

Toby glanced sideways at the speaker. He was a man of around sixty, with thinning black hair and a pale face, flushed at the cheeks. There was a hint in his features that he had once been an attractive guy, but the years had gradually wiped away the sheen of beauty. He was wearing a heavy, dark overcoat, but from his concave cheeks and skeletal hands, Toby could tell he was extremely thin.

"What is it?" Toby mumbled, sitting upright and looking around the carriage. It was empty, apart from the man and a pretty black woman and her young son sitting several seats away. The child was eating snacks out of a bag that were leaving crumbs everywhere and staining his lips yellow. He grinned at Toby. Toby tried to smile back but discovered he didn't have it in him to even pretend to be happy.

"Your wallet has fallen out of your pocket," said the man, waving the leather accessory in front of Toby's face. "Also, the next stop is the end of this line, so I thought I'd better wake you."

"Shit," said Toby taking the wallet and resisting the temptation to make sure nothing had been taken from it. "Thanks, mate."

"No problem. Did you sleep through your stop?"

"Yeah. I meant to get off at Angel." Toby yawned and rubbed his eyes.

"I'm just visiting an old friend in Edgware," said the man, standing as the train drew into the station.

"Nice," said Toby. "Thanks again for this." He pushed the wallet into his back pocket.

"My pleasure," said the man. He surprised Toby by holding out his hand. "My name's Albert Darkwater, by the way. I popped a card in your wallet, just in case you are ever looking for new accommodations. I rent rooms in a very desirable property right on Hampstead Heath."

Toby laughed as he gave Albert's hand a quick shake then pulled himself into a standing position using the vertical bar next to his seat. "I can only just afford the crappy little flat I have in Islington, never mind a desirable property in Hampstead. But thanks."

"You may be surprised," said Albert, heading for the nearest door as it slid open and the recorded voice warned everyone alighting from the train to '*mind the gap*'.

"I doubt it," said Toby, following Albert onto the platform and searching for an information board that would tell him how long he had to wait for a train that was going back to Angel.

"All the rooms are very affordable," said Albert. "My late mother stipulated in her will that the house was only mine if I continued her legacy of making Darkwater House accessible to those on lower incomes."

"Hey…" said Toby, suddenly feeling irritated with Albert. *What right does he have to put a card in my wallet?* "I'm not on a low income. I'm on a pretty decent income. I'm a freelance journalist. I've had stuff in *The Times*. London is expensive, that's all, and Hampstead is one of the most expensive addresses in London, so I'm pretty certain I can't afford any rooms in Coldwater House — or whatever it's called."

"I didn't mean to offend," said Albert, pausing at the foot of a flight of steps.

Toby took a deep breath and smiled. "No, I'm sorry," he said. "It's not been a good day so far. Thanks again for being so honest and for the card."

Albert nodded, swiveled on his heels like a palace guard and headed up the stairs to the exit.

When Toby finally arrived home some forty minutes later, he let out a moan at the state of his flat. It smelled of old cooking and damp, there were two empty wine bottles lying on the floor next to the couch and there were peanuts scattered all over the carpet. He really had started early the previous night.

That was one of the dangers of working from home. If he wasn't that busy, the wine started flowing as early as four o'clock in the afternoon. And, despite what he'd told Albert, he hadn't been that busy for a few months. Freelance journalists were two-a-penny now, and his work had been getting sloppy since he'd begun drinking so much.

Someone knocked at his front door. Toby groaned again. He knew it would be his stoner neighbor, Luke. Luke was nineteen years old and dealt drugs on a small scale to make some extra cash on top of his state benefits. He was a sweet guy, but when he came over, Toby was always subjected to an hour or more of Luke rambling on while he puffed on a joint. Normally his visits were late in the evening, after his slightly older girlfriend had fallen asleep and he wanted to stay up smoking. Toby didn't mind listening to him drone on when he was drunk himself—Luke was cute to look at, although totally straight—but the last thing Toby wanted now was company. He remained standing just inside the door, not moving and trying not to breathe too loudly, hoping Luke would assume he was out, or asleep, and shuffle back to his flat and its permanent fog of smoke.

"Hey, bro," his neighbor called from the other side of the door. "Just heard you come in. You feel like a chat, man?"

Toby sighed and opened the door, planning to explain that he was exhausted and now was not a good time, but Luke, dressed in a hoodie and a pair of striped boxer shorts, slipped past him into the flat and threw himself onto the nearest armchair. He looked at Toby through hooded eyes. A stray blond curl had escaped from the gray hood of his top, spilling across his line-free forehead. Like his delicate facial features, his pretty blond curls were totally at odds with his laddish personality.

"How you doing, bro?" he asked, his legs falling open so that his boxers rose up to reveal the tops of his milky white thighs.

Toby experienced a rush of lust. Although Luke was far from being his normal type, in his hungover state, there was something sexy about this straight teen lounging in his flat in his underwear.

"I'm shattered, to be honest, Luke," said Toby, not sitting, hoping Luke might get the hint and leave if he remained on his feet.

"Too bad, bro," said Luke. At least he wasn't smoking. The flat smelled bad enough without Luke's habit adding to the mix.

"I was just about to hit the shower then get some sleep," added Toby.

Luke nodded and gave his crotch a lazy grope. "No problem, man. Do your thing. I'm chilled."

Toby couldn't help but stare between Luke's thighs, watching as he stroked his genitals through his shorts. He wasn't usually *this* relaxed. He was suddenly looking at Toby through slitted blue eyes.

"I don't mind if you want to suck it," he said.

"What?" Toby was genuinely taken aback.

"As long as you don't want me to suck you back, bro... No way could I suck a cock, man. But I don't have a problem with you wrapping your lips around mine. I'll just sit back and enjoy it. I could close my eyes and imagine you're my girl."

"Luke, do you even know what you're saying?" asked Toby, growing hard despite his efforts to think unsexy thoughts. He already felt sullied after his experience waking up with Joe. The last thing he needed to add to the list of things he regretted was having sex with his straight, nineteen-year-old neighbor while his girlfriend slept across the landing.

"Yeah, man, I know what I'm saying. I'm horny and Zoe ain't putting out."

"So, you thought you'd pop over to your gay neighbor and get him to oblige," said Toby.

"Are you going to?" asked Luke, massaging his cock more urgently now. His boxer shorts were tenting and a small damp patch of pre-cum had formed on the front of them.

Toby realized this was a pivotal moment in his life. The old Toby would have been crawling across the living room floor now and taking Luke's cock into his mouth, enjoying Luke's guttural groans as he brought him to orgasm, but Toby didn't want to be that person anymore. He wanted to shower, sleep and start life again when he woke up.

"Luke, I'm tempted, but I need to sleep," he said, focusing on Luke's face rather than his bulging boxer shorts.

"Seriously?" asked Luke, frowning.

"Yeah. I need to get to bed."

Luke shrugged, stood with surprising speed and ambled to the front door. As he walked, his erect cock pushed through the opening in his boxer shorts, displaying a shining head, moist with pre-cum. Toby sighed and hastily looked away. He was only human. Any more temptation and he would just give in.

"Take care, Luke," he said, opening the door.

"You too, bro," Luke replied, and Toby closed the door behind him before he had a chance to reconsider.

His heart beating rapidly, he headed to the small bathroom, hesitating in front of the mirror.

"Jesus," he whispered at the sight of his face. Nothing had improved in the past two hours. There were dark bags under his bloodshot green eyes and dry flecks of skin on his full lips. He was only twenty-six, but today he looked more like forty.

He stripped, noticing that his once-flat six-pack was starting to fade a little, and his thighs were less toned than they had been a few months before. He needed to stop drowning himself in wine and get back to the gym. He ran a hand across his smooth chest then through his collar-length dark hair and stepped into the shower. As the water gushed over him, he tried to convince himself that he was washing away everything he had said and done in the past twelve hours.

Chapter Two

For the first time in weeks, Toby woke on a Sunday morning without a hangover. He was in his own bed and alone. There were no empty wine bottles littering the floor and the flat smelled of furniture polish and bleach. He'd spent the previous day—when he'd finally gotten up—cleaning the flat, metaphorically washing away the past, ready for his new start.

"Today is the first day of the rest of my life," he said to his reflection in the full-length mirror inside his wardrobe door.

Just one day off the booze and he already looked better. His face was no longer as puffy, and the bags under his eyes were a lot lighter. He stroked a hand down his body from chest to groin, playing with his semi-erect cock for a moment, admiring his reflection.

He'd hit the gym later—just half an hour or so on the cross trainer and some fixed weights for now, but it would be a start.

As he dressed, he noticed the business card that Albert Darkwater had given him lying next to the bed.

He remembered looking at it the night before then tossing it onto the floor. He picked it up and studied it properly for the first time. One side displayed Albert's full name — Albert Archibald Darkwater — and a phone number written in a fancy italic font. On the reverse was an image of a white building, probably built in the sixties. It wasn't what Toby had expected from Darkwater House. He'd imagined a Gothic pile, not this relatively modern, five-story block. It looked cool, though — the kind of place a wealthy young couple in the swinging sixties would have had built. He found it hard to believe that Albert Archibald Darkwater's parents had fit that description, though.

Written in the same italics across the image was the declaration — *Affordable accommodations in an idyllic setting.*

Still clutching the card, Toby wandered from the bedroom to the living room, surveying it like an estate agent. It was tidy now, but it was still a dump. If today really was about new starts, maybe he should at least go to see Darkwater House. No doubt it would be way out of his price range, no matter what Albert had said. He had probably lived off his parents' inheritance for years, with no idea of the cost of living for normal people like Toby. But at least ringing the number and popping over to see the room would show that he was serious about starting again. Plus, Hampstead was a beautiful part of London. After he'd seen the room and confirmed it was too expensive for him, he could go for a walk over Hampstead Heath. Perhaps today he would get his exercise that way, rather than going to the gym.

As was his way, Toby prolonged his decision, heading to the café below his flat to ponder the future.

It had once been an old-fashioned working man's café, selling cooked breakfasts and builders' tea, but a year ago it had been bought by a brother and sister who had gentrified it, and it now offered vegan and gluten-free options of everything, along with a selection of specialty teas and coffees.

Siobhan, one of the owners, was working behind the counter when he entered. She gave him a quick appraisal and grinned. "Late night?"

"Actually, no," replied Toby, sliding into a chair as far from any other diner as possible. "I thought I was looking pretty fresh."

"Are you eating or just having coffee?" she asked, coming over to his table with her notepad and pencil in hand. She flicked her long, dark hair out of her eyes and waited, pencil poised.

"I'll get a Brie and salad sandwich and a large white coffee," said Toby. "Then if you can tell me what to do with the rest of my life, I'd be very grateful."

Siobhan laughed. "Oh gosh, it's like that, is it? Let get your order and I'll see if I can help."

Toby was a regular at the café and he and Siobhan always chatted when she wasn't too busy. Unknown to her, Toby had once had sex with her younger brother and co-owner, Caleb. He was a short, slim guy with brilliant green eyes and wavy black hair. He was around twenty-three, maybe younger, and married to a pretty Scottish woman. One night Toby had bumped into him at the Black Swan pub and they'd begun chatting. Caleb had confessed to being attracted to guys as well as women, and an hour later, he'd been fucking Caleb doggy style. Toby had a vivid flashback of Caleb's cute little arse when he crouched on the bed, begging Toby to fuck him hard.

Although they had seen each other often since, he'd never mentioned it and neither had Caleb. It was a fun memory, though.

"So, what's the deal?" asked Siobhan, placing his order in front of him and taking the chair opposite.

"I want to change," said Toby after a gulp of coffee, which burned his mouth.

"What's wrong with the way you are now?" asked Siobhan.

"I drink too much, sleep around too much and yesterday I woke up in my ex's bed on the other side of London with no memory of how I got there," said Toby.

"Okay," said Siobhan, nodding.

"So, I really do need to make some changes, and I was thinking a move might be a good start. Some guy gave me this card on the train yesterday." He handed Albert's card to Siobhan. "Apparently it's an affordable accommodation right on Hampstead Heath. Seems too good to be true, but I was thinking of calling."

Siobhan studied the card and handed it back to him.

"If it sounds too good to be true — "

"It probably is," completed Toby.

"But there's no harm in looking into it," continued Siobhan. "Just be on your guard in case it's some kind of scam. How did the guy who gave you the card seem? Did you get good or bad vibes?"

Toby considered this. "Both," he said, finally. "He was very kind and seemed genuine enough, but there was something behind his smile that I didn't like. I wasn't in the best state at the time, though."

"So, maybe it is worth calling and seeing what he has to say," said Siobhan, standing. "Go with your gut feeling. That's all I can really advise. That's what I did when I decided to open this place, and it's working for me so far."

Another diner called for Siobhan's attention and she gave Toby a sympathetic smile before heading over to their table.

Toby stared at Albert's card for a moment. *I've got nothing to lose*, he thought, fishing his cell phone from the pocket of his jeans and dialing the number.

* * * *

Darkwater House was set on a narrow slip road right on the edge of the heath. Toby couldn't see the property from the street, as it was surrounded by a tall brick wall and an even taller row of trees. But he knew for sure, now that he had seen just how close to the heath it was, that he would never be able to afford to rent a room there, even if it was the size of a shoebox and infested with rats. Houses in that area sold for around eight million, and this was a big property. The rental value would be huge, even with the generous discount Albert claimed he would offer.

Putting those thoughts aside for the moment, Toby studied a panel next to an austere wooden door set in a larger gate, which was designed to allow access to vehicles. There were nine buttons in total — some blank, others bearing names. The bottom button bore the name Darkwater, so Toby pressed it. There was a crackle of static, then Albert Darkwater's voice asked, "Is that you, Toby?"

"Yes, it's me, but I have to warn you —" Toby began.

There was a click and the door opened. Toby had his first glimpse of Darkwater House. The image on the card had been a flattering one. While the building was expansive and still retained some of its original sixties vibe, it looked tired, as if it had enjoyed the swinging sixties a bit too much and continued to party into the next few decades. The once-white façade was more a tarnished yellow with obvious streaks of damp, where water had dripped from the lip of the flat roof down the walls for years. Much of the ground floor was comprised of tall windows, and as Toby approached down the sloping driveway, he saw that these were coated in dirt, with the odd sweeping patch of clear glass where someone had made a half-hearted effort to clean them.

A middle-aged man and woman suddenly came through the gate behind Toby. They were rowing, which had caused Toby to glance back. The woman, dressed in a shapeless blue raincoat, was red in the face from shouting and the plump man was jabbing a finger close to her face and telling her to "shut your stupid mouth!"

When they saw Toby, they fell silent and looked embarrassed. Toby offered a weak smile and turned back toward the house.

The front door, set on the far right of the building, opened and Albert stepped onto the gravel driveway, giving a thin smile. He held out a bony hand and Toby shook it reluctantly. It felt cold and clammy. The couple passed between them into the hallway, their argument put on hold, at least for now.

"Welcome to Darkwater House," said Albert, whose teeth were as discolored as the walls of the house. He ushered Toby into the hall, which stretched the width of the property, with large windows at either end. Directly in front of the door was a stairway, the carpet a shade of gray. The floors of the hall were covered the same. Toby guessed it hid the grime. Next to the stairs was a small lift, just about big enough to hold two people — and next to that a narrow passage.

"That leads to my rooms," said Albert, gesturing toward the passage. "If you ever need anything, just knock."

Toby opened his mouth to explain that he already knew he wouldn't be staying, but Albert stepped into the lift and waited for Toby to join him. Albert smelled of cologne, the kind Toby's dad wore, but he seemed to have doused himself in it. As the lift door closed, Toby immediately felt uncomfortable. His crotch was pressed against Albert's thigh, and he couldn't change position without actually rubbing himself against the old man. He wondered if Albert was aware of this inadvertent intimacy. The other man wasn't speaking, which somehow made the experience of being so close even more embarrassing. Toby remained rigidly still until the lift finally clunked to a stop on the fourth floor. The door took an age to open. Toby almost leaped out onto the landing. Albert coughed and followed him.

"This way," he said, and Toby followed him along a corridor. They passed just one other door before stopping outside apartment number eight.

"Here we are," said Albert, reaching into the pocket of his gray trousers. Toby cringed at the obvious bulge that still filled Albert's crotch, even after he'd removed the set of keys. It seemed Albert had enjoyed their trip in the elevator a little too much.

Albert pushed open the door to flat eight and gestured for Toby to enter first. He stepped into a long, narrow hallway running both to his left and right. Directly ahead lay the door to the living room, which was open. Toby looked back at Albert, who nodded.

The living room was huge, at least twenty-five feet by twenty, and the wall opposite the door was almost entirely covered in windows that were surprisingly clean compared to those on the ground floor. And the view was spectacular. Toby walked slowly over to the nearest window, shaking his head in disbelief at just how beautiful a scene lay before him. The property was practically on Hampstead Heath. Trees reached over the perimeter wall as if clutching at the house, and beyond them was an expanse of meadow, then more woodland. And in the distance, he could see Parliament Hill, with a multitude of brightly colored kites soaring above it.

"Quite a view, aye?" said Albert, resting a hand on the small of Toby's back, brushing his little finger against Toby's arse. Toby stepped sideways to dislodge the hand. He noticed three dead flies lying on the windowsill. Obviously, whoever had cleaned the apartment to ready it for viewing hadn't been too fastidious.

"I could never afford somewhere like this," Toby said, averting his gaze from the dead insects back to the stunning view.

"What do you pay for your current accommodation?" asked Albert.

"One thousand two hundred a month," said Toby.

"This is yours for eight hundred," said Albert, smiling.

Toby laughed. "No way! You could get thousands for somewhere with a view like this, even if it is a bit run down. Why would you let me have it so cheap?"

Toby paused, thought of the cringe-worthy trip in the elevator, the bulge in Albert's trousers and the hand on his back and decided that he knew exactly what the deal would be.

"Albert, other than the money, would you expect anything else for my rent?"

Albert frowned then tutted, gripping hold of the nearest window ledge for support, as if the very suggestion had made him feel faint.

"You mean would I expect sexual favors?" he asked, sounding breathless. "Absolutely not. I gave you my card because I thought you were someone who would benefit from living here. Don't ask me how. I just have a bit of a sixth sense for these things. But if I'd known you were going to make such lurid assumptions, I would never have bothered."

"Please," said Toby, resting a hand on Albert's shoulder, which stiffened at his touch. "I'm so sorry. It just all seems too good to be true. I didn't know places like this and people like you and your late mother existed."

"So, you want the flat then?" asked Albert.

Toby smiled. "You haven't given me the grand tour yet," he said.

"The bedroom is this way," said Albert, turning back toward the narrow hall. "As long as you won't think I'm leading you there for sex."

Albert glanced over his shoulder and the knowing leer on his face made Toby think he wouldn't say no if sex was offered, however much he protested.

As Toby passed the front door to the apartment, he heard heavy breathing from the corridor outside. He chanced a quick look down the passage and saw a guy standing outside the door nearer to the elevator. He was dressed in running gear—a loose-fitting black vest top and shorts. Even from this distance, Toby could see the muscle definition of his legs and arms. He glanced in Toby's direction as he pushed his front door key into the lock. For a brief moment they made eye contact, and Toby took in the handsome tanned face and cropped black hair. The man, who Toby guessed to be around his age, looked hastily away and let himself into his flat without offering a smile.

"Are you coming?"

Toby jumped. Albert was standing inches from him, his mouth so close to Toby's that Toby felt the warm breath on his cheek and smelled stale garlic.

"Sorry," said Toby, forcing himself not to flinch away, "I got distracted."

"No point lusting after him," said Albert, sounding almost gleeful. "He's not queer. He just split up from his girlfriend. He's totally broken-hearted about it, poor man. He only moved in a few weeks ago. Sometimes I hear him sobbing."

"Poor guy," said Toby, knowing that later as he showered, he'd masturbate while thinking of the handsome stranger who might be his new neighbor.

Chapter Three

Toby moved into flat eight, Darkwater House, Hampstead a month later, just as autumn had begun to turn the heath into a beautiful landscape of golds and reds. He couldn't believe his luck. Sure, the flat was sparsely furnished, and what furniture it did have was tatty and at least thirty years old, plus there was a large damp patch in the kitchen and he thought he might have seen a mouse scuttle across the bedroom on his first night. *But look at that view, and all for eight hundred pounds a month.* A deal like that really was worth giving Albert Darkwater an occasional blow job for, not that any such suggestion had been made. They had even taken the stairs back to the ground floor after Albert had finished showing him the apartment, as if his landlord had wanted to avoid any more intimacy and misunderstandings.

Anyway, I'm not the kind of guy who gives old men blow jobs for cheap rent – not anymore, thought Toby, flopping onto the sofa and choking on the resulting cloud of dust. He really needed to give the place a thorough cleaning.

He'd even turned down sex with Luke, his former neighbor, a second time before leaving his old flat. This time Luke had actually pulled out his cock and gripped it in his small fist, pretty much begging Toby to suck it, claiming his girlfriend just wasn't into giving head. But Toby wasn't that guy anymore, and he'd said no then sent Luke on his way.

He was also not the guy to get drunk on his own several times a week and end up sleeping with his exes or complete strangers. He'd had the odd glass of wine since his epiphany, but never enough to get drunk. He wasn't an alcoholic, just someone who had established bad habits and needed a fresh start.

And Darkwater House was that new start. Despite its grimy façade, creepy landlord and air of faded grandeur, it had something very special about it besides the incredible views.

Special but also spooky, whispered Toby's subconscious, but he ignored it. Yes, he'd noticed a slightly weird atmosphere when he'd first viewed the house — not so much in his flat, but in the communal areas. It was as if someone were watching...and assessing.

That's ridiculous, he scolded himself. *Stop trying to turn something good into something bad.*

And speaking of good things, he hadn't seen the hot guy from along the corridor since he'd moved in, but he'd thought about him a lot. On his first evening in the new flat, he'd stripped naked and lain on the sofa, wanking as he gazed out of the window, thinking about his neighbor in his tight black shorts, fantasizing about kneeling in front of him as he stood with his key in the lock to his front door, pulling down those shorts and breathing in the smell of fresh sweat, taking the guy's thick, hard cock into his mouth and swallowing it to the root. He'd come in several powerful gushes before the fantasy could progress any further.

But now the vision of the gorgeous runner came back to him — his moody stare, those muscular arms and legs and his pert butt, displayed to perfection in his shorts. Toby grew hard and massaged his dick through his jeans. Maybe he should just pop over to the guy's apartment to introduce himself. It would be the neighborly thing to do. But the memory of that hostile gaze made Toby reconsider. Fantasizing was one thing, but that look had not been an inviting one. Somehow that all just made him more attractive, and Toby pulled his cock out through his now-open fly and began to jerk off again. This time he took longer, careful not to come before he had stripped his fantasy lover naked and shed his own clothes. They fucked in the corridor, Toby letting his neighbor take him from behind, pushing him against the door to his apartment, their bodies pounding against the wood.

Just as orgasm began to encroach, someone rang the bell to his flat. Toby swore and gripped the base of his cock until his orgasm subsided, creeping backward and taking that wonderful warm feeling with it.

It was Albert who stood in the corridor — not, as Toby had hoped, his sexy neighbor.

"I brought you this to say welcome to Darkwater House," said the old man, holding out a bottle of red wine. "I meant to bring it yesterday, but there was a particularly exciting episode of *The Great British Bake Off* and it completely slipped my mind."

Toby looked at the bottle, considered refusing it and saying he didn't really drink, but suddenly the cold glass was clutched in his hand and he was thanking

Albert for the kind gesture. He hoped his landlord wouldn't expect to be invited in to share the offering.

"Don't forget to call if there is anything you need," said Albert. "Did you get the Wifi sorted?"

"Not yet," said Toby, "but an engineer is coming tomorrow to fit a router. Reception here is terrible, so it will be good to get it up and running."

"Jolly good," said Albert, edging backward. "Well, enjoy the wine."

As Albert walked back toward the lift, the door to flat seven opened and the handsome runner stepped into the corridor, once again dressed in black shorts and a vest top. Toby hovered in his doorway, drinking in the sight of his beautiful neighbor, reliving his fantasy of earlier, aware of the pre-cum leaking through his briefs from the wank that had been cut short.

"Good evening, Sean, how are you?" asked Albert as he passed the man.

So, now Toby had a name—*Sean*. It suited him. When he next fantasized about him, Toby could murmur that name to himself as he jerked off.

"Hi," Sean replied to Albert. "How are you?"

He had a soft Irish accent and his voice was deep and masculine.

"Muddling along," called Albert, disappearing around the corner.

Toby took a deep breath and said, "Hi, I'm your new neighbor."

Sean looked in Toby's direction and nodded, before heading toward the stairs.

That went well, thought Toby, closing his front door with a sinking heart.

He considered opening the wine, but instead put it inside one of the kitchen cupboards. There was something satisfying about hearing the cupboard door click closed.

It was Friday night, however, so he wanted to do something with his evening. Work was still slow, so he couldn't afford a big night out, plus he still wasn't on speaking terms with any local friends, although that was a situation he planned to rectify now that he was getting his life back on track. What he really wanted to do was take the bottle of wine around to his hot neighbor, but that was not a realistic option. He could just picture Sean's shocked and probably repelled expression on seeing Toby at his front door suggesting a cozy night in together.

Instead he resolved to go the nearest supermarket and buy some comfort food—maybe some ice cream and a pizza. As he reached the lift, the door slid open and a woman of around sixty almost fell out. She was struggling with several carrier bags—and judging from the clanking of bottles, she had bought a large quota of alcohol for the evening.

She looked surprised to see him, as if encounters like this were rare. Then she glanced around and swore.

"I'm on the wrong sodding floor," she said, then the bottom of one of the bags split and two wine bottles clunked to the ground and a tub of ice cream landed on Toby's foot.

"Sorry," said the woman, chasing after the escaping items, depositing a bottle into each pocket of her knee-length overcoat and turning her apologetic gaze on him. Toby smiled, proffering the ice cream.

"Comfort food?" he asked, immediately regretting it.

The woman took the tub, blushing. She had very pale skin, Toby noticed, and very dark hair, obviously dyed. Her eyes were outlined in dense black, the lids a vibrant green. She was actually quite exotic-looking.

"I'd better get these things put away," she said, stepping back into the lift.

"Can I help?" asked Toby. It just seemed like the right thing to say.

The woman looked unsure, but politeness ruled so she smiled and handed him two of the bags. "Thanks, if you're sure."

After a short struggle with the lift door, which had closed the second the woman stepped out onto the third floor and now seemed reluctant to open, no matter how many times Toby pushed the appropriate button, they made it to the woman's floor. She'd told him she was in apartment six while they had been in the lift. The woman immediately went inside.

"Hello!" he called, standing in the doorway, not liking to walk in uninvited.

From this vantage point, he could see that almost every inch of wall space in the hallway was covered in movie posters, theater flyers and signed pictures of actors. Just inside the door, slightly overlapping a huge poster of Betty Blue, was a postcard-size signed photo of Dame Judi Dench, and a few feet along from the Dame was Jeremy Irons, looking characteristically somber, and just by the living room doorway, Nanette Newman.

"Nanette Newman?" said Toby. Her name was printed on the picture, otherwise he would have had no idea who she was.

"She was signing them for charity," said the woman, appearing in the kitchen doorway. "I felt obliged. I'm Susan, by the way – Susan, not Sue."

"Toby," he said and held out his hand. Susan gave it a dainty shake, using the very tips of her fingers. She smelled of rich perfume, which, Toby now noticed, swamped the room.

"Thanks for helping with the bags," said Susan, relieving Toby of the two he'd carried.

Toby assumed this to be a dismissal and took a step backward.

"You can have a glass of wine if you'd like," said Susan. As she spoke, she returned to the kitchen. Toby felt the usual mini thrill at the sound of wine glugging into a glass.

Susan reappeared and handed him a full glass of red, indicating with a nod that he should follow her into the living room.

"Was it a bad breakup?' Susan asked as she wafted over to one of the Chesterfield sofas that formed a right angle in the center of the room.

"What?" Toby froze.

"Oh, sorry... Albert said something about you being single and that he thought you'd recently split up from someone," said Susan, waving a hand at the other sofa.

"No breakup for me," said Toby, feeling angry at his slimy landlord for gossiping about him—and getting it wrong. "Not a recent one, anyway."

"Most people here have either just broken up from someone, lost a loved one or gone through something miserable," said Susan. "Not that any of us really talk much... Albert fills me in."

"Do you work?" asked Toby, taking a gulp of wine. It was good.

"I'm a failed actress and a failed wife and mother."

Toby wasn't sure what to say to this, so he took another gulp of wine.

"I almost made it several times," continued Susan, "but something always went wrong. I nearly got a part in *Four Weddings and a Funeral*, but my agent fell out with the casting director. I was screen-tested for *Moulin Rouge!*—the musical version with Nicole and Ewan—but I was too old, apparently. Too old to play a hooker."

"I interviewed her once," blurted Toby.

"Really?" Susan looked surprised.

"I'm a journalist. I've done a few celeb pieces. Nicole was nice."

"Sorry," said Susan, and she seemed to soften, to physically seem less angular.

"What for?" asked Toby, goblet of wine held to his mouth.

"I'm talking about myself. It's not because I'm hideously self-centered. I just get nervous when I meet new people and feel I've got to impress them. I had a date once, years ago, and I ended up doing a performance of *Cabaret* for him before we'd even left for the restaurant—not just the song, the entire musical. I'd had a few too many drinks before he arrived to collect me."

"Don't worry,' said Toby. "I get insecure too. I get insecure about being single sometimes. I always feel I have to justify why I am."

"Why are you?" asked Susan.

"It's a long story," said Toby.

"I'm not rushing off anywhere," said Susan.

Toby noticed her gaze at his lap for a moment and wondered if she was hoping for more than a chat.

"Such a shame you're gay," she said. "I'd love to have a passionate affair with a handsome younger man."

Toby laughed. "I'd like to have an affair with Sean, the guy who lives on my floor. Have you seen him?"

"Black hair, always in running gear?"

"That's him."

"Gorgeous," said Susan, fanning her face with her hand.

Now they both laughed.

"Top up?" asked Susan, and Toby nodded. Having a few drinks was fine when he was in company.

By the time Toby got back to his own floor, he and Susan had consumed three bottles of wine between them. She was actually quite entertaining. And she talked so much that Toby had been able to concentrate on just drinking. As he staggered toward his apartment, the door to flat seven opened and Sean stepped out into the passageway. He was dressed in tight blue jeans, a white polo shirt and a black leather jacket. Toby stared at the bulge in his jeans, remembering all his fantasies about sucking on that obviously big cock.

"Take a picture, why don't you," said Sean, slamming his door and heading for the lift.

"Sorry," called Toby, inwardly cringing.

There's definitely not going to be any passionate affair with that man, he thought.

Chapter Four

The first thing Toby recalled the next morning was the drunken encounter with Sean. He'd only been at Darkwater House a couple of days and already he was failing to make his fresh start. This morning felt like so many others had. His head throbbed, he was exhausted before he'd even got out of bed and he was filled with regret. How was he going to face Sean now? Every time they passed in the hallway it would be awkward, Toby having to stare at the carpet to avoid eye contact.

After his first coffee, he began to feel a little better about the situation. All he'd done was stare at Sean's crotch. It was not quite a major offense. Susan had stared at his bulge and he hadn't got all funny about it. Why did Sean have to be such a prick? Surely he could see that Toby was pissed. Why couldn't he have been his usual taciturn self and just nodded or scowled?

As Toby sat at the small breakfast bar in the kitchen sipping coffee, he thought of Sean's well-packed crotch and his perfect little butt in those skinny-fit jeans, as he'd strutted with attitude toward the lift. Toby grew hard and groped himself through his boxer shorts, which was all he was wearing.

This was also a familiar scenario, the hangover horn. However tired he felt after a night of heavy drinking, he almost always felt desperate for a wank—or sex, if there was someone else around. There certainly wasn't anyone close by who he could call on for sex, although he was sure Albert would jump at the chance to suck his cock. The thought of the creepy landlord gobbling at his dick almost quelled his horniness, but soon his thoughts returned to Sean—those dark eyes, toned arms and legs, that arse squeezed into tight jeans and always so moody.

'Take a picture, why don't you?' In that sexy Irish brogue.

Toby leaned back in his stool and pulled his cock out through the opening of his shorts. He admired it for a moment—seven inches of uncut dick—then began to jerk, thinking of Sean peeling off those jeans, revealing tight white briefs, the head of his cock poking above the waistband, already dripping with pre-cum.

Toby groaned and shot cum across his stomach and chest.

He'd needed that.

"Oh dear," came a voice from the hall. "Is this a bad time?"

"Shit!"

Albert was standing in the kitchen doorway, his face a vibrant shade of red. Toby leaped to his feet, fighting to push his cock back into his shorts and aware that he was covered in cum.

"I did knock," said Albert, making no attempt to look away.

"Could you step out into the main hallway for a minute?" snapped Toby. "I need to get my dressing gown."

"Of course," said Albert, backing away. "I was just letting this gentleman in. He's here to set up your Wifi. He couldn't get an answer from your intercom and I knew you wouldn't want to miss him."

Toby almost bumped into the engineer who was standing in his hall, clutching a metal case and looking mortified. He'd obviously picked up on what had happened. At least he had the decency to look at the floor. He was actually quite handsome, in a rugged, older man way, although Toby was too embarrassed to dwell on that as he hurried to the bedroom.

When Toby returned to the living room, having cleaned himself up and pulled on a dressing gown, Albert had gone and the engineer was busy setting up the router in the far corner near one of the large windows. He glanced over his shoulder as Toby entered and he grinned.

"Sorry about that," he said. "I think you gave your landlord a treat, though."

Toby blushed. His initial appraisal of the engineer had been correct. He was a very handsome forty-something guy, with cropped blond hair speckled with gray. His chin and cheeks were covered in stubble and his smile was warm and appealing. Where he was crouching, Toby also had a view of his wide arse, which stretched the bottom half of his blue overalls to the limit, the deep crevice between the no-doubt-rock-hard cheeks clearly visible.

"I don't know why the intercom didn't work," said Toby. "I'll get Albert to check it. I didn't hear him knock."

"You were busy," said the engineer with another grin. "This is almost done. I have time for a quick coffee if you're putting the kettle on."

Toby surprised himself with his response. "I'm sorry, but as soon as you're done, I need to shower and head off for a meeting."

"No problem," said the engineer, turning back to his task.

Normally Toby would have jumped at the chance of spending time with a sexy guy, flirting with him to test his boundaries, maybe opening his legs so that the engineer could see his tenting boxer shorts. But he'd only just come, and even the hunky engineer couldn't eclipse Toby's feelings of lust for his neighbor.

Toby hurried to the kitchen and poured himself some juice. That was the kind of thing the old Toby would have done. This was the new Toby, even if he had slipped back into his old ways the previous night.

No more casual sex with strangers.

Toby laughed. The engineer was probably just a typical straight guy who enjoyed teasing gay men. When he'd said coffee, he'd probably just meant coffee.

"I'm done then," the man said behind him, making Toby jump. "Any problems, just call the main help desk."

The engineer was standing very close. He smelled faintly of sweat and a brand of very masculine aftershave.

"Thanks," said Toby, hastily showing him to the door. Suddenly, he was sure the stocky guy would be up for more than just a coffee.

The engineer winked and smiled before heading toward the lift. Toby considered calling him back and offering a coffee after all. What would be wrong with some no-strings sex with an attractive older man? He imagined lying with his legs open and the engineer climbing on top of him, his thick cock rubbing against Toby's, staring down at him with those twinkling eyes. But he took a deep breath and closed the front door. He would go for a long walk over Hampstead Heath, clear his head and shake off his hangover.

And within an hour, that was what he was doing. He'd discovered a path at the side of the house that led directly onto the heath. At the end of the path — or more accurately, narrow mud track — he had to descend a steep slope onto a beautiful overgrown meadow. He could have been in the middle of the countryside. It was hard to believe this was London. He didn't see another soul until he reached a main path, winding between densely packed trees, then he was surrounded by people — and dogs. Every breed of canine imaginable was walking on the heath that morning. A huge Great Dane gave him a look that suggested he knew exactly what Toby had been up to, while a chirpy little terrier grinned to let him know he was going to be fine.

I'm going mad, thought Toby.

He followed the path for around twenty minutes, already feeling his mood lift. Eventually, he came to a large duck pond with a grass slope stretching its entire length, dotted with people, many sitting on the grass despite the chilly weather. It was cold but bright, with autumn light streaming through the trees that dotted the bank. He took a path that led up the slope of the bank then turned left. He had no idea where he was going, but figured he'd eventually discover a spot he recognized and find his way home from there.

After a few minutes, he passed the women-only bathing pond, with a sign reading 'No Men Beyond

This Point' fixed to a wooden fence. He could hear laughter and the odd yelp as someone hit the freezing water, but the pond was screened by mature trees to protect the privacy of its bathers.

A female jogger huffed and puffed her way along the pathway toward him, her ponytail bouncing behind her. Another jogger followed a few yards behind. It was a man, dressed in black shorts and a vest top. *Sean.*

Toby panicked and tried to find somewhere to hide, but the wooded area to his right was fenced off and on the left was a high wall that ran for much of the length of the pathway. As Sean drew closer, Toby looked at the ground and kept walking. Maybe Sean wouldn't notice him.

"All right?" came the gruff voice of his neighbor as he jogged by.

Toby glanced up just in time to meet the other man's gaze. Sean nodded and raised an eyebrow but didn't stop.

Progress.

Perhaps Sean wasn't such a dick after all. Maybe he'd realized that he had overreacted the night before. Tomorrow he'd be asking Toby around to his apartment for a drink and one thing would lead to another, and they'd be naked in bed together with Sean sliding that big cock of his inside Toby.

Yeah, right, thought Toby, bringing his latest fantasy to a halt. He didn't want to spend the rest of his walk with a raging hard-on. He needed to stop obsessing over this guy and focus on sorting his life out.

His walk took him through the Kenwood Estate and past Kenwood House, a stunning neo-classical villa. He thought about stopping and having something to eat at the café there — or maybe exploring inside. He seemed to remember there was a collection of landscape paintings that were worth seeing. But he was starting to feel tired and fancied a couple of hours just relaxing in his new home.

It took him more than half an hour to find his way back to the meadow that was behind Darkwater House. As he prepared to climb the slope leading to the back of the house, he spotted someone standing by the high brick wall. He squinted against the sun to try to get a better look. It was a female, wearing a long green dress and what looked like a gray shawl. Voluminous red hair was billowing around her face. The sun was suddenly very bright and Toby closed his eyes against the glare, just for a second or two. When he opened them, the woman had gone. Toby shivered, not sure why she had made him feel uneasy, and he was keen to be home in the warmth.

Chapter Five

Toby thought about the strange figure he had seen for much of the day, still unsure why the woman had made such an impression on him. His unease almost eclipsed his feelings of lust for his neighbor. Although, every now and then, the memory of the red-haired woman in the green dress would be pushed aside in favor of one of Sean jogging past, sweat running down his forehead, black shorts clinging to his butt. But before long, the image of the strange woman would be back, and he would shudder again and gaze out across the heath for comfort. She was just a woman. There wasn't even anything unusual about her, apart from her voluminous red hair. But for some reason, Toby related her to that slightly spooky atmosphere that clung to the communal areas of Darkwater House.

As dusk fell, he decided to head to the nearest shop and buy some food for the evening. He thought of the bottle of red wine in the kitchen that Albert had given him. It was Saturday night, so surely he was allowed a bottle of wine. He wouldn't buy any more.

When he returned to Darkwater House half an hour later, he held a carrier bag containing a chicken curry ready meal, some poppadoms and a bottle of merlot. It had been on special offer, so it had seemed a shame not to get it. He could hold on to it until next weekend.

He entered the code into the electronic keypad next to the main front door and waited for the now-familiar click before pushing it open. Sean was standing in the communal hallway, his back to Toby, bending forward so that the material of his running shorts stretched across his muscular buttocks, revealing a tantalizing crack. God, Toby would have liked to smell that arse, run his nose from one end of the crevice to the other, taking a long, deep breath.

Stop it!

Sean was rubbing his right calf. Toby hesitated, then cleared his throat.

"Are you okay?" he asked, still staring at Sean's butt while he had the chance.

Sean straightened and looked over his shoulder at Toby.

"I think I pulled a muscle," he said, hobbling toward the lift.

Toby considered taking the stairs to avoid an embarrassing trip in the compact elevator, but instead followed Sean and pushed the button for the fourth floor.

"Is it painful?" he asked, breathing in the smell of Sean's fresh sweat, reveling in the closeness of the other man. He could feel heat radiating from his post-exercise body.

"A bit," said Sean, staring ahead. "I think I overdid it today. That was my second run."

"I know. I saw you this morning," said Toby. In his head, he was slipping a hand down the front of Sean's shorts, playing with his flaccid but growing cock, his hand getting slippery from Sean's sweat and pre-cum.

Then I'd lick my fingers, he thought.

The lift pinged and the doors opened.

"After you," said Toby.

Sean nodded a thank you and walked awkwardly toward his flat. Toby followed, fixing his eyes on the other man's butt, growing hard and once again fantasizing about burying his face between those cheeks, breathing in the masculine scent.

"See you later," said Sean as he reached his apartment door, resting his gaze briefly on Toby's face.

Toby blushed. "Yes, see you later. I hope your calf gets better."

As he headed for his own flat, Toby wished he had some sort of medical training so he could have offered to check out Sean's injury, maybe administer a gentle massage on the injured leg. The thought of his hands caressing Sean's muscular calf, rising to his thigh, Sean watching him intently with his dark eyes, was all too much. Toby hurried to open his front door, pulling his cock out of his fly almost before the door had closed behind him. He jerked himself fast, still clutching the carrier bag of food and wine in the other hand. Several jets of cum shot across the hallway carpet. *I'll have to clean that up later.*

Toby fell back against the front door, breathing heavily, pushing his cock back into his pants. He really did have it bad for Sean, even though they'd barely spoken and Sean seemed to dislike him, or at best, be indifferent toward him. Or perhaps that was the attraction? If he fell for someone he stood no chance with, he wouldn't get hurt like he had before, because nothing would ever develop.

He dropped the carrier bag onto the kitchen surface and pulled out the bottle of wine he had bought at the supermarket. He studied it as if it were some ancient relic of great interest, rather than a cheap bottle of plonk. Then, with a sigh, he unscrewed the top and reached for a glass. It was Saturday night, after all, he told himself.

One bottle of wine down, Toby began to feel horny again. He craved company, perhaps some casual sex. He tapped on the cruising app on his phone and scrolled through some of the nearby guys looking for hook-ups. No one appealed. Plus, he didn't like using apps. He always found the waiting stressful. Would they fancy him? Would he fancy them? At least if he met someone face-to-face in a bar or club, he'd know there was a physical attraction. But he couldn't afford to go to a club and didn't fancy sitting on his own in a bar tonight.

He opened the second bottle of wine, the one Albert had given him, and slumped back onto the couch, feeling fed up and still randy. Sean had a lot to answer for.

As he gulped back the fresh glass of red, sinking into a drunken haze, he had an idea.

Why not head to the gay cruising area on the heath?

The heath's cruising zone was legendary among the London gay community. Toby had never visited but had heard all about it from many of the older patrons of The Black Swan pub. The area was situated on an extension of the heath, separated from the main expanse by a major road junction. Toby knew where it was and it was only around a five-minute walk from

Darkwater House. The more he thought about it, the more appealing some anonymous sex seemed. A quick blow job among the bushes – no chat, no need to even see their face. That was all part of the turn-on. In the dark, he would have no idea if he was sucking the dick of a god or a ghoul. Maybe he'd let a stranger suck him off. Who cared what they looked like? He'd just enjoy the sensation of a pair of lips around his shaft, a tongue teasing his cockhead, then come all over their face before zipping up and heading home.

Darkwater House is meant to be a new start, the sensible voice in his head objected, but the red-wine-soaked part of his brain had other ideas.

Go on! Live a little!

* * * *

Toby stumbled as he made his way down the sloping pathway to the heath extension. He knew the path led to a narrow dirt track between the trees and that if he turned left off that track, he would be in the cruising area. A taxi driver had pointed out the path to him a few years back, not long after he'd moved to London.

"That's where all the queers go," the driver had said, "just behind Jack Straw's Castle. Avoid that bit of the heath, unless you want a nasty surprise."

Jack Straw's Castle was an imposing building set on the main road. Up until a few years ago it had been a pub – the one-time hang-out of Charles Dickens, no less. Now it was a block of luxury apartments.

Toby reached the mud track and the trees swallowed up the light from the streetlamps some two hundred yards behind him. *Do I really want to do this?*

He felt suddenly anxious and pined for his living room and the comfy sofa. But he pushed any doubts aside and plunged into the woodland to his left. Up ahead, he could see shadowy figures milling around the trees and bushes, like ghosts doomed to wander for eternity. Toby pushed that thought from his head, too and tried to focus on the pleasure of getting or giving an anonymous blow job. He'd be home in no time, feeling relieved and relaxed. He'd finish the second bottle of red and fall into bed.

A dark figure approached him, feet crunching through the crisp leaves on the ground. As the stranger drew close, Toby saw that he was in his fifties at least, his face doughy and red. The darkness didn't obscure people's faces as much as Toby had imagined. The man reached out and cupped Toby's balls.

"No," barked Toby, and the man walked on without comment.

Others were approaching from all sides now, shadow men of all shapes and sizes, drawn to this new, young arrival. Toby began to panic, slipping between the nearest two and delving deeper into the woodland.

He paused by a tree, leaning his back against it, trying to be invisible for a while. He felt overwhelmed, even a little scared. There was so much sex on offer, but it felt too primitive somehow, the way the men had approached him from all sides. What next? Would they start sniffing his arse like dogs would?

When did you get so judgmental? he asked himself.

What was wrong with wanting sex and coming here to find it?

He pushed away from the tree and began walking again. Another man brushed past him, looking back at Toby over his shoulder and nodding. Toby could just about make out a clean-shaven face, high forehead and short, dark hair. From behind, the guy looked stocky, his arse wide, with sturdy thighs like those of a rugby player.

Why not?

He followed the stranger into a clump of shrubbery. There was already a couple hidden there, one man on his knees while the other stood almost motionless, gently groaning. In the little thicket, it really was too dark to see what they looked like, and Toby was focusing on his stocky stranger.

The guy with rugby-player thighs grabbed Toby's hand and pulled it toward his crotch. Toby gasped as he touched the man's solid cock. This guy wasn't wasting any time on small talk. But that was the general idea.

After a moment's hesitation, Toby took a firm grip on the thick shaft and sank to his knees. He licked the stranger's cockhead, tasting a hint of pre-cum, before wrapping his lips around it and slipping them over the swollen glans, then pulling back with a slurp. The man moaned appreciatively. Toby was aware of the couple next to them. The guy on his knees was just inches from where Toby crouched, and the one being serviced stood very close to the stranger whose cock Toby was sucking. As Toby continued to feed hungrily, his attention kept wandering to the other standing figure. He was hidden by darkness, but Toby could tell from his shadowy outline that he was tall and lean, and the guttural groans he was releasing as his orgasm grew closer were turning Toby on more than those of the man he was currently engaged with. He wondered if the pair would embrace a foursome, offering him the chance to taste the other stranger's cock. But as the thought occurred to him, the object of his desire let out a long, low moan, and something warm and wet hit Toby's face. He might not have gotten to give the other stranger a blow job, but apparently he had taken the brunt of his cum explosion. As Toby relished the sensation of the treacle-like liquid running down his cheek, the knob he was slurping on also exploded and more creamy cum filled his mouth. He swallowed, caught up in the sordidness of the situation — one man's cum covering his face, another's slipping down his throat.

His stocky lover was already zipping himself up and backing away.

"Cheers, mate," the man said, heading off into the night.

The other pair were also fumbling to zip up and stand, talking in muffled voices.

"Thanks for that," the standing man said to the one who had been kneeling. Toby suppressed a gasp. The voice was familiar — *that soft Irish accent.*

Toby stood, wiping the stray cum from his face with the sleeve of his coat. He backed out of the clump of bushes but loitered, waiting for the guy with the Irish accent to start walking back toward the path up to the road. As he emerged from the bushes, Toby followed a few yards behind.

The man was walking with a slight limp. As he reached the path and the distant streetlamps offered some illumination, Toby saw the short, almost-black hair and the familiar slim, muscular physique, that perfect arse… It was Sean. He was sure of it.

Chapter Six

By the time Toby reached the foot of the path, the figure ahead was more visible as he grew nearer to the light of the main road. Toby quickened his pace, closing the gap between them. As the man stepped into the full glare of the streetlights, Toby was in no doubt that it was his neighbor. He could now clearly see the other man's profile, and he'd fantasized enough about that face to know Sean when he saw him. His grumpy, hot neighbor was not so straight after all—and he'd just inadvertently come all over Toby's face.

Toby's heart bounced and his stomach churned with warm delight at the memory of the thick jets of liquid hitting his cheek. Now that he knew it was Sean's cum, the incident held even more erotic power.

Red wine and adrenaline propelled him forward. He was going to confront Sean, admit that he'd been kneeling in the same clump of bushes, perhaps even show him the sticky cum on the sleeve of his coat where he had wiped his face and tell Sean that it was his.

He was just feet away from his neighbor, about to announce his presence, when thunder struck and the sky erupted into a ferocious downpour of rain. Sean instantly broke into a run, his injured calf slowing him to a jog rather than a sprint, but still opening up the gap between himself and Toby.

Toby cursed and began to trot after Sean, his view of the other man already obliterated by the spears of rain pounding the ground between them. By the time he reached Darkwater House, Toby was drenched. He punched the code into the panel next to the outer gate and ran down the path. Sean was at the front door, entering the second code needed to gain entry to the house. He glanced at Toby but said nothing, pushing open the door and bolting through without holding it open. Toby managed to slip inside before it closed. Sean was standing by the elevator, cursing and dripping wet. He was dressed in the same tight-fitting jeans as the previous night and the rain made them cling to his arse and thighs more snugly than ever, so that every curve and crevice was defined. Once again Toby was overwhelmed by the fact that this beautiful man's cum had recently soaked his face. His cock stirred as he approached the lift and stood next to the object of his lust.

The elevator arrived with a ping and the door slid open. A young woman with light brown skin and jet-black hair jumped slightly at the sight of them. She was wearing a nurse's uniform and looked extremely morose. She said an almost inaudible "Hi" as she slid past them and headed for the front door. She swore at the severity of the weather outside, but opened it and bolted up the path.

"Rather her than me," said Toby, squeezing into the lift beside Sean, who said nothing.

Suddenly Toby felt irritated by the other man's unsociable, rude behavior, making out he was too macho to talk to his gay neighbor when five minutes ago he'd been groaning with pleasure while another man sucked him off.

"Did you have fun over on the heath?" Toby blurted, once again spurred on by the red wine still coursing through his system. "You sure sounded like you did."

Sean snapped his gaze onto Toby's face. He looked shocked and furious in equal measure.

"What are you talking about?" he demanded, his accent made stronger by anger.

"Just now, in the bushes," said Toby, "I was the guy kneeling next to your...friend."

Sean jabbed at the button for the fourth floor. His hand was shaking.

Toby lifted up his right arm, shoving the cum-stained sleeve under Sean's nose.

"Thanks for the facial," he said, "even though it wasn't meant for me."

The lift pinged again and the door opened at the fourth floor. Sean stepped out and turned to glare at Toby.

"Fuck you!" he shouted, before striding to his front door.

"I'd settle for a blow job, but if you insist, I could go for a fuck," said Toby, following just a few feet behind. "I've always been versatile, so happy to return the favor and slip one up your tight arse too."

Toby didn't even see the punch coming before Sean's fist hit his chin. He yelped in pain and toppled backward, landing heavily with a loud grunt. Air left him in one painful woosh.

"Stay away from me," said Sean, stepping into his apartment and slamming the door behind him.

Toby lay staring at the ceiling, feeling stunned and sluggish from the punch and alcohol. As he hoisted himself into a sitting position, he heard sobbing coming from the far end of the corridor. It sounded like a woman, and there was something eerie and crazed about the tone of it. It was a horrible repetitive sound, like something recorded and played on a loop.

Toby's vision was still spinning, but when he squinted, he could make out a figure standing in front of the large window that filled the far wall of the passageway. It was the red-haired woman he had seen that morning—it had to be—but tonight she was dressed in funereal black and her face was aged and skeletal. Even from this distance, Toby could see the madness in her eyes. As he watched, the terrifying figure rose from the ground and began to float toward him, like some ghost-train apparition, still wailing, black dress billowing around its insubstantial frame.

As the horror loomed above him, Toby screamed and closed his eyes. When he opened them, it was Sean looking down at him, not the ghostly woman, and for once he didn't look aggressive. He looked concerned.

"Are you okay?" he asked, reaching out a hand.

Toby accepted the offer of assistance, too shocked by his brush with the supernatural to appreciate that he was finally making physical contact with Sean.

"I'm sorry I belted you," said Sean, releasing Toby's hand.

"No, I went too far," said Toby, glancing up and down the corridor for any sign of the ghostly woman.

"I still shouldn't have hit you," said Sean, looking at the floor like a shamed child.

"It's okay," said Toby. "I shouldn't have embarrassed you. I'm a bit drunk and I was over-excited at seeing you there and everything else. I won't mention it again. It's none of my business."

"Thanks," said Sean. "Your lip is bleeding. Do you need any cream to put on it?"

Toby shook his head. "I'll be fine. G'night."

"'Night," said Sean, backing into his apartment and closing the door.

Toby felt suddenly fearful. What if the woman returned now he was alone? Who the hell was she? And why was she focusing on him?

He hurried to his own front door, struggling to fit the key in the lock with his quivering hand, but finally managing.

What a night.

Once inside, he headed straight for the kitchen and the still-half-full bottle of wine. He filled a glass and drained it, then poured the rest of the bottle into the same glass and took it through to the living room.

He fell onto the sofa, recent events spinning through his mind.

Sean liked men. Sean had come on his face. Sean had hit him. A dead woman had terrorized him. Sean had apologized. It was a lot to take in.

Despite the enormity of the evening, Toby's eyes began to feel heavy, and he placed the half-full glass of red wine on the old packing case that acted as a coffee table and went to bed. His dreams were plagued by visions of the hideous apparition, but also blessed with lustful moments featuring Sean, his cock standing proud between those sculptured thighs, pumping out jets of warm cum into Toby's waiting mouth.

* * * *

By the time he'd drunk his second coffee the next morning, Toby had convinced himself that the confrontation with the ghost had been a hallucination brought on by too much wine and the punch to his jaw. How else could it be explained — unless he was actually going to accept the existence of spirits? He hadn't believed in ghosts since he was a kid. The woman he'd seen after his walk on the heath had obviously been some local eccentric, and his mind had stored up the image of her and replayed it while he was reeling from Sean's attack.

He felt rancid and was glad he had no work to do that day — although he needed to find some soon, even with the savings he was making on rent.

Someone knocked on the front door. Toby groaned. He was not in the mood for a visit from creepy old Albert. But when he opened the door a crack and peered out, it was Sean who stood in the passageway, still wearing his concerned expression.

"Oh, hi," said Toby, suddenly aware that he was dressed in just a pair of boxer shorts and a T-shirt, and probably looking like death warmed up.

"I just wanted to check that you were all right," said Sean, his voice stirring the lust in Toby, despite how awful he felt, "and to ask if you fancied coming for a walk — if you're not too busy. I can't run because of my pulled muscle, but I want to get some exercise."

Toby hesitated. There was nothing he wanted more than to spend time with Sean, however badly things had gone the night before, but he also thought he might need to throw up, which wouldn't make a great impression.

"You're busy," said Sean. "Don't worry. Why would you want to come for a walk with the nutter who punched you in the face? I'm sorry. I'm an idiot."

Toby laughed. This was a dramatic change — from taciturn to overly chatty in the space of around ten hours.

"I'd love to come for a walk," he said, "but can you give me half an hour to have a shower?"

"Sure," said Sean, and he grinned.

Toby had to hold in a gasp at the sight of Sean's face lighting up with a smile. If he'd been handsome as a grumpy sod, he was beautiful when he was happy.

"I'll knock for you," Toby said, pushing the door closed and punching the air with joy. It had taken nearly getting knocked out, but Sean had thawed.

Chapter Seven

At first, conversation was stilted and Toby wondered if he'd been too quick to celebrate. Sean seemed to have returned to his more-reserved self, delivering one- or two-word answers to all Toby's questions. Toby was considering addressing the events that were, no doubt, contributing to the awkwardness, but Sean surprised him by being the one to do so.

"I guess we should talk about last night," he said, as they reached the main pathway, which today was relatively quiet and dog-free.

"Okay," said Toby, feeling shy now that he didn't have a bottle-and-a-half of red wine inside him.

"Obviously I like guys as well as girls," said Sean, staring straight ahead.

"But you haven't ever come out as bisexual?" ventured Toby.

Sean shook his head. "I never felt the need to. I've not had a proper relationship with another guy. It wouldn't feel right." He finally looked sideways at Toby. "I don't mean there's anything wrong with it. It just isn't me. I've only ever been out with girls. Sex with guys is just...well, sex. I enjoy it and everything, but there's never been any emotional attachment."

"Did you have sex with men while you were with your ex-girlfriend?" asked Toby.

"No," said Sean, "never while I was with Jess, but with other girlfriends I did. I never really thought of it as being unfaithful. It was another me that was doing stuff with guys. It was just a bit of fun, something to do in the shadows, if you like."

"I see," said Toby, already calculating whether he could enjoy a purely sexual relationship with Sean. It could be perfect — no emotional involvement, just sex. Lots and lots of sex...

"So, tell me about some of your past conquests," said Toby.

"You mean blokes?" asked Sean, glancing behind them, obviously to check that no one was close enough to hear their conversation.

"Yeah," said Toby, wanting to hear every detail but knowing Sean wouldn't be that open.

"Well, there've been a few. There was one lad who used to walk past the bus stop I waited at in the mornings. Every day he'd give me a look and eventually I started looking back. He was cute — not much older than twenty, nice arse, long dark hair, a bit of a hippy, I guess. Anyway, one morning I followed him, he slowed down, we started chatting and he invited me to his place. He worked nights as a hospital porter and had just finished his shift. I decided to be late for work that day, then I ended up taking the day off. That guy loved getting fucked, that's all I'm saying. My poor dick was sore by the evening."

Toby was surprised at Sean's graphic description and wanted to hear more. His stomach was churning with lust, but Sean glanced around again and looked regretful, as if he wished he hadn't shared so much.

"I really don't want people knowing," he said, once again looking at Toby.

"Who am I going to tell?" asked Toby.

"Albert?" suggested Sean, and they both laughed.

"He is such a creep," said Toby.

"He tried it on with me the day I moved in," said Sean, "Put his sweaty little hand on my arse while I was bending over to put something in a drawer."

"Did you hit him?"

Sean let out a nervous laugh. "No, I just told him never to touch me again or it would be the last thing he ever did. He's been good as gold since. I think the poor old git is lonely."

"Aren't we all," blurted Toby. *Why did I say that?* He didn't want Sean feeling sorry for him. But Sean didn't respond. They walked on in silence for a while, although it was no longer awkward.

Eventually they reached the end of the path and stood facing the duck pond.

"Which way?" asked Sean.

"Shall we head to the top of Parliament Hill?" suggested Toby. "Take in the view."

"Sure," said Sean, leading the way along the path that ran around the right-hand side of the pond.

Parliament Hill — or Kite Hill, as it was also known — offered an incredible view of London, with the skyline incorporating the old and the new. The ultra-modern, jagged spire of The Shard and the historic dome of Saint Paul's jostled for space with the BT Tower and Canary Wharf. Toby stood close to Sean as the two of them stared out across the heath to the horizon. It would have felt so natural to take hold of Sean's hand at that moment. Well, it would have felt natural for Toby, but he was pretty sure Sean wouldn't be comfortable with the scenario. Toby wasn't about to find out, although his fingers itched with the desire to do so.

"It's a grand city really, isn't it," said Sean.

"I love it and hate it," said Toby. "How long have you been here?"

Sean thought for a moment. "Since I was twenty, so six years. I was brought up just outside Dublin. My father was Dublin-born-and-bred and my mother came from Bradford. Her parents were from Pakistan. She met my dad while she and some mates were in Dublin for a wild weekend. They got chatting and discovered they were both teachers…and things went from there. They dated for about six months then Mum moved to Ireland and they were married. Her family didn't come to the wedding. They never had anything to do with her again. It's sad, but I've never met that side of my family."

"Are your parents still alive?" asked Toby.

"God, yeah," said Sean. "Very much alive and still acting like bloody newlyweds."

"That's nice," said Toby. "Mine split up when I was fifteen. Dad lives in Manchester now. Mum is still in the house I grew up in, near Slough."

"Slough, aye," laughed Sean. "No wonder you moved this way."

"Yeah, it's not the most exciting place to grow up."

"Do they know you're gay?" asked Sean as they began to descend the hill, neither having to suggest moving on.

"Yeah. I came out a few years ago, when I met my first serious boyfriend. Well, my only serious boyfriend."

"Were they okay about it?"

"Mum was fine. Dad took a while to get his head around it. He's a builder — and a real bloke, if you know what I mean. But he's cool with it now, not that I see him that often."

"I'm not sure how mine would react if they knew I sometimes play around with guys."

"I guess you don't need to tell them if you've no intention of ever dating another man," said Toby, indicating that they should turn right at the bottom of Kite Hill.

"Exactly," said Sean. "Why complicate things when I don't need to?"

"What do you do for work?" asked Toby, deciding a change of subject might be in order.

"I'm a carpenter by trade," said Sean, "but I got fired from the last building firm I worked for. I lost the plot a bit when me and Jess split up and missed a lot of time off work. My boss wasn't too sympathetic. I'm trying to build up a freelance business, but it's not proving to be easy."

"And how did you end up living at Darkwater House?" asked Toby.

"I was living in a shitty little basement flat in Camden when I bumped into Albert in a café one morning," replied Sean. "I was hungover and feeling like shit. He sat at the same table as me and started chatting. At first, I just wanted him to shut up and piss off, but something about him made me open up. I can hardly remember what I said, but after he'd gone, I found his card on the table. Christ knows why I rang the number. How the hell was I going to be able to rent a flat in a place like Darkwater House when I could barely afford a crappy little studio flat? But I'd told him about my situation, so he knew I had no income, just a few thousand in savings. Anyway, he assured me the rent would be more than reasonable and that I should come and view the apartment." Sean paused. "Sorry… I'm wittering."

Toby chuckled. "You certainly weren't guilty of that when we first met."

"Yeah, sorry about that. I just get nervous when hot guys show an interest."

"I only said 'Hello'," laughed Toby.

"Yeah, but it was the way you said it," said Sean. "And there's that hungry look in your eyes."

Sean flashed his delicious smile and Toby flushed, the warmth spreading from his face down his neck.

"Do you fancy a pint?" asked Sean. "I really fancy a pint."

"Why not?" said Toby. "We can cut through South End Green and walk up to the King William."

"Isn't that a gay pub?" asked Sean.

"No, not anymore," said Toby. "There's no need to panic, Mr. In-the-Shadows."

For a second Sean looked serious, then the gorgeous grin split his face and Toby was happy, despite the hangover, and the unease he still felt over his hallucination of the previous night.

* * * *

The King William was busy, as always. It was one of Toby's favorite London hang-outs, although he hadn't visited for a year or so. When he'd first had a drink there, it had been much more gay but never pretentious. It was a local pub with a local crowd, now very much mixed. The walls were adorned with photos of celebrities with a Hampstead connection, and the furniture was an odd assortment of tables and benches, possibly collected over a number of years from various junk shops, all giving the bar the feel of some eccentric old aunt's living room.

Sean kept glancing around, as if unsure it was his kind of place. Or perhaps, considered Toby, he wasn't comfortable being seen with a gay man in the daylight. Maybe he was regretting his suggestion of a drink.

Sean drained his pint of lager and released a satisfied sigh. Toby's wineglass had been empty for the past half-hour, but Sean hadn't offered to refill it and it was his round. Toby was now even more convinced that Sean was having second thoughts about their new friendship.

"Well, thanks for the company," said Sean, shifting his chair back. "And thanks for being understanding. I really wouldn't want anyone to know about, you know, what you saw last night."

Sean looked around the pub, as if fearful he might be overheard.

Toby had a sudden moment of realization.

"Is that what today has been about?" he asked. "Making sure I won't drag you out of the closet?"

Sean placed a finger to his lips and made a hushing sound, while glancing around the pub again. He actually looked panicky now.

"No," he whispered, taking his jacket from the back of his chair and pulling it on as he stood. "I wanted to show you that I wasn't a total bastard. I felt bad for hitting you."

"Consider your debt paid," said Toby, also standing, and wondering how the day had taken such a bad turn. "No need to humor your gay neighbor anymore. No one will hear from me that you like getting your cock sucked in the bushes."

"Shut up!" hissed Sean, and the old look of anger and resentment had returned to his face.

Toby headed for the nearest exit. Sean followed close behind.

"Please, Toby, don't kick off." Sean placed a hand on Toby's shoulder.

"I'm fine," said Toby. "I just don't like being patronized. Let's just go back to me saying 'hello' and you grunting at me."

Sean pulled Toby to a halt. "I don't want to do that," he said, staring intensely into Toby's eyes. "I enjoyed today, and I'd like us to be mates."

"Great," said Toby.

"You just made the word 'great' sound like 'fuck you,'" said Sean.

Toby began walking again. "I need to get back too," he said. "I have a feature to write."

They strode on in silence—once again awkward—until they were a few yards from the outside gate of Darkwater House. A man of around twenty-five was standing on the narrow pavement. He appeared confused and upset.

"Can I help you?" asked Toby as they drew closer.

The man looked at him, flustered. "I was meant to see my mum today," he said, "but she isn't answering. I spoke to the landlord and he said she went out first thing."

"Who's your mum?" asked Toby.

"Susan Hooper," the stranger replied. "Do you know her?"

"I think so," said Toby. "Is she in flat six?"

"Yes, but I've been ringing her intercom for ten minutes. I've tried her mobile phone and she isn't picking up."

"If I see her, I can let her know you were here," offered Toby.

The guy nodded, seemingly resigning himself to the fact he wasn't going to see his mother today. "I'd appreciate that," he said. "She probably passed out with a bottle of wine still clutched in her hand."

Toby wanted to say something in Susan's defense, but he barely knew her, and her son was already marching away.

"That's strange," he said, punching in the security code and pushing open the gate.

"She must have forgotten he was coming," said Sean.

As they walked down the path to the house, Toby saw a figure standing inside the hall near the window that was next to the front door. As they drew closer, he realized that it was Albert, but he couldn't work out what the old man was doing.

"Oh, hello!" greeted Albert. As they entered, he jumped backward and put his hands behind his back, as if to conceal something. He glanced from Toby to Sean, frowning, then he seemed to remember himself and the frown turned into an insincere smile. "Making friends?" he asked.

"Something like that," said Toby.

"I was just checking that the intercom was working," said Albert, although no one had asked. "A couple of tenants have missed callers recently, apparently, but it all seems fine."

"Was Susan's working okay?" asked Toby. "Her son was just here."

"Yes, I spoke to him," said Albert, edging backward toward the passage that led to his apartment. "She went out this morning. She seemed a little...worse for wear, shall we say."

"It's a shame she missed him," said Toby.

"Yes," agreed Albert. "Well, take care, both of you. I need to get on."

Albert scuttled down the corridor to his flat.

"Such a creepy guy," said Sean.

"How do you know he hasn't sucked you off in the dark over at the heath?" asked Toby, stepping into the lift, his finger poised by the button for the fourth floor.

"I'll take the stairs," said Sean. "Give my calf a stretch."

Toby watched him walk away until the lift door closed.

As the lift rose, Toby pondered the last part of the time he'd spent with Sean and wished he hadn't got testy with him. He'd fantasized about Sean for days then blown any chance he had of getting closer to him. If he'd played his cards right, they could have been enjoying another drink in Sean's apartment right now. Toby could have raised the idea of them being mates with benefits, and a few drinks later, he could have had his head between those toned thighs. Instead, he was heading back to his flat alone, and there was no feature to write.

When the lift door opened at the fourth floor, Sean was waiting for him. Toby tried to --hide his delight.

"I didn't want to leave things like they were," said his neighbor. "Why don't you come and have a coffee at mine."

Toby smiled. "Sure," he said. "I was feeling bad too. I don't know why I got so grumpy."

"I have that effect on people," said Sean, leading the way to his flat.

As he ushered Toby inside, Sean placed a hand on his shoulder again. "I really did enjoy today," he said, and kissed Toby on the back of the neck.

Toby froze. He had not expected that.

"Sorry," said Sean. "I didn't mean to upset you."

Toby turned to face him. "You didn't," he said. "I was just surprised."

"Why?" asked Sean, smiling. "I told you I thought you were hot."

"I know, but I thought…"

Sean silenced Toby with a kiss. Toby was so taken aback that he didn't return it, but instead took a step backward. Sean looked confused.

"Have I totally misread this?" he asked.

"No," spluttered Toby, "I fancy you, you know that, but I didn't think you felt the same, and I didn't expect you to want to kiss, not after everything you said earlier."

Sean laughed. "Why would I not want to kiss you? You're fucking cute. I meant what I said. I'm not looking for anything serious, but I'm up for a bit of discreet fun."

Toby's mind was racing. Wasn't this what he'd wanted? His hot neighbor, the guy he'd been fantasizing about since he'd first laid eyes on him, was offering him sex on a plate. Why was he hesitating?

"I need to get back to mine," he said, hardly believing the words were coming out of his mouth. "I really need to do some work."

Sean shrugged and stepped to one side so that Toby could leave. "No problem," he said.

"Sorry," said Toby, turning back as he reached his front door. But Sean's door was already closed.

Toby cursed and thumped the wall with a clenched fist. Why had he chosen now to get all self-righteous? Last night he'd been on his knees sucking off a complete stranger and taking a faceful of cum from Sean, even if he hadn't known it at the time. Today he was getting all prissy about having some fun with a man he genuinely liked.

Maybe that was the problem. Perhaps he already liked Sean a bit too much. He'd resigned himself to the fact that if anything did happen between him and Sean, it would just be raw sex based on nothing but lust. But when Sean had kissed his neck, it had felt affectionate. Toby had experienced a rush of something more than just lust, and he'd panicked.

As he opened his front door, Toby thought he heard someone crying—a woman. He strained to work out where it was coming from, but it was too faint.

Chapter Eight

Toby spent the first half of that evening trying to convince himself that he didn't need a glass of wine. By seven o'clock, he'd lost the argument and pulled on his coat, ready to head to the shop.

He was on his way back—tell-tale carrier bag in hand—when he heard the screaming and realized it was coming from Darkwater House. He hurried the rest of the way down the road to the outside gate and hastily entered the security code. As he pushed the gate open, he saw a small crowd gathered near the front door. The only people he recognized were Albert, the nurse who he'd seen the night before and the rowing couple who he'd encountered on the day of the viewing. As he approached, the nurse crouched down next to a bundle of some kind lying on the ground. Not a bundle, he realized, a person.

Oh Jesus!

He took in the floral-patterned dress and the heavily bejeweled hand, which lay at an odd angle to the wrist it was attached to. The women's legs were jutting out of the floral fabric in weird positions, like those of a doll that an angry child had discarded. Toby directed his gaze to the woman's head — or what was left of it. There was hair and flesh and bone, but it barely resembled a human head anymore. Even so, he was sure it was Susan from flat six. He turned away, feeling faint and nauseous. Someone else was throwing up just to his right.

He stumbled toward the nearest wall, needing to lean on something before he fell. The world began to spin and he let out a groan.

"I've got you," said someone — not just someone, Sean. And arms were suddenly wrapped around him, holding him upright, a bristled face pressed against his and a soft Irish voice whispered, "It's okay, just breathe."

The world came back into focus but, for a few seconds, Toby remained in Sean's tight embrace, letting the warmth of the other man's body seep through him. Once again there was affection in Sean's intimacy, and Toby was feeling more than lust as he clung to him. Finally, he pulled away, nodding a thank-you. He was touched by Sean's kindness. It had to have taken a lot for him to show tenderness toward another man in front of an audience, although maybe he was aware that everyone's attention was on poor Susan's body, not them.

"Are you sure you're all right?" asked Sean.

"Just shocked," said Toby. "What happened?"

"I'm guessing she jumped from the roof," said Sean. "I saw her falling past my living room window. It scared the life out of me. Then I heard someone screaming and came down to see what the hell was going on. Poor woman."

"It's Susan," said Toby. "I spent the other evening with her. She was nice. It was her son who we met earlier."

"Right," said Sean, glancing at the body.

"I've called an ambulance," announced Albert. "I suggest you all go back to your rooms and leave me and Gita to deal with this."

Toby assumed Gita was the name of the nurse, who had stood up, obviously recognizing a lost cause when she saw one. She looked even more miserable than she had the previous night.

Toby surveyed the other onlookers. There were the unhappy couple—neither offering the other any comfort—and across the body from them, a stocky black guy, probably in his thirties. He wore round-framed glasses and was clutching a paperback book. Next to him was a young woman dressed in jeans and T-shirt, hugging herself against the cold. She looked devastated. Judging from the strange stains on her shirt, Toby guessed she had been the one throwing up.

"I live next door to her," she said. "I didn't realize she was so unhappy. I wish I'd made more of an effort to talk to her. I feel awful."

She looked around at the others, but no one offered her any reassurance that she wasn't to blame.

"Come on," Sean said to Toby. "I'll see you back to your flat and make sure you don't pass out on the way."

Toby didn't argue. He did still feel wobbly.

In the lift, Sean draped an arm around Toby's shoulder, which felt pleasantly affectionate and made Toby blush. He hoped his redness would be attributed to his queasiness over the accident rather than embarrassment.

"You feeling okay now?" asked Sean.

"I'll be fine. I just need to sit down," replied Toby as the lift door pinged open.

"Let me make you a cup of tea before I go back to mine," offered Sean, as Toby fumbled to fit the key into the lock of his front door.

"You don't have to," said Toby, finally succeeding in opening the door.

"I want to," said Sean. "Sit yourself down and relax. I'll find everything."

Sean was already busying himself in the kitchen, so Toby did as he'd been told, lounging on the sofa with a quiet sigh.

What could have been so bad in her life that Susan would have thrown herself from the roof?

He thought about her son trying to get hold of her and his confusion that she wasn't at home or answering her phone. Had she been considering suicide even then? Was that why she hadn't wanted to see him?

Then Toby remembered Albert loitering by the front door. What had he been doing? And why had he been so quick to explain himself, as if he were up to no good?

The intercom system for Darkwater House was in two stages. There were buttons for each flat next to the outside gate, then a second set next to the front door of the house. If someone had a visitor, they either had to meet them at the main front door or their guest would have to ring again once they were outside the house. *Are the two intercom systems connected?* wondered Toby. Could Albert have tinkered with the intercom for Susan's apartment from the hallway?

Why am I even thinking like that? What reason did he have to suspect Albert of deliberately sabotaging Susan's meeting with her son?

And yet, now that he had considered it, he couldn't stop thinking it was a possibility. Maybe that was why Albert had been hanging around by the front door. He claimed he'd been checking the intercom system because he'd had complaints it wasn't working properly, but what if he'd been tampering with it to disconnect Susan's buzzer so that she would miss her son's visit? Maybe she'd told him she was expecting her son that afternoon. But why would Albert want to prevent them from seeing each other?

"Here you go." Sean was standing over him, holding out a mug of tea.

Toby jumped. He'd almost forgotten Sean was there.

"I didn't know if you took sugar or not, but I put one in. On TV, people always drink sweet tea when they're in shock. I have no idea why."

The warm mug was comforting and the close presence of Sean's crotch just inches from his face was also pleasing, for very different reasons. He could clearly see the outline of the other man's cock through his tight jeans. He remembered again the feeling of warm cum hitting his face over the heath and, despite the recent trauma, he grew hard.

He pushed the ridiculous thoughts of Albert from his mind and focused on the situation at hand.

"Why don't you stay for a bit?" he suggested. "I have some wine."

"That would be cool," said Sean. "But I have some beer at mine, so I'll nip over and get that. I'm not much of a wine man."

"Great," said Toby. "You can go get it now. I'll be fine."

The sound of sirens rose up from the road. Toby pictured Albert scuttling up the drive to open the main gate to let the ambulance and maybe police car through. He was filled with a feeling of intense dislike, which made no sense. Albert had been good to him. Sure, he was a bit creepy, but Toby had a huge flat with the best view possible at an impossibly cheap rent, thanks to him. He shouldn't be feeling anything but gratitude.

"Are you sure you feel better?" asked Sean.

Toby looked up into Sean's dark eyes and nodded.

"Go get your beer," he said.

* * * *

To begin with, Sean sat in one of the living room's two armchairs, while Toby remained on the sofa. But when Toby returned from the kitchen at around nine o'clock with a fresh glass of wine, his guest had moved to the couch, one arm draped across the back, legs crossed at the ankles, which seemed to emphasize the bulge in his jeans. Toby hesitated before sitting next to him—but only for a second or two.

The sofa was only a two-seater, so Toby found his thigh resting against Sean's. His neighbor didn't seem to object. At least, he made no effort to shift away.

"Cheers," said Sean, clinking his can against Toby's glass. "Thanks for forgiving me. I'm sorry I was such a moody bastard when we first met."

"Don't worry," said Toby. "It kind of turned me on, to be honest."

The red wine was kicking in.

"Did it now?" said Sean, looking sideways at Toby with a grin.

"I didn't exactly hide the fact that I fancied you," said Toby, hoping he wasn't saying too much, but he was also relaxed enough not to stop.

"The feeling's mutual," said Sean. "Just in case I hadn't made that clear."

Sean dropped his arm from the back of the sofa onto Toby's shoulders. Toby's heart stopped beating for a second then began pounding like a bass drum. He was sure Sean must be able to hear it and feel it. The whole sofa must have been vibrating.

"Am I going to be one of your secret encounters in the shadows?" Toby asked as he put down his wine and met Sean's gaze.

"I'm happy to keep the lights on," said Sean, and he leaned forward, placing his glass on the table then planting a kiss on Toby's lips. And this time Toby did respond, opening his mouth and welcoming Sean's tongue. The kissing grew increasingly passionate, Sean gripping the back of Toby's head with one hand while the other slipped under his T-shirt. Toby's skin tingled with warm pleasure. He rested a hand on Sean's thigh, digging his fingers into the hard muscle. The other he placed on Sean's chest, which was as firm as stone.

Toby slid his hand from Sean's thigh to his crotch, gripping his erect cock through the material of his jeans, running his fingers along its impressive length then sketching the outline of the swollen head. He was so turned on that it was almost too much to bear. His own cock was so hard it hurt. He broke the kiss, taking a deep breath and staring into Sean's brown eyes. He was about to say something he would probably have regretted later when someone rapped on the door.

Toby swore and Sean let out a despondent sigh.

"Who is it?" called Toby, still gripping Sean's bulge.

"It's the police," a female voice replied. "We're just talking to all the residents about tonight's incident."

Toby gave Sean's cock a final squeeze and Sean kissed him once more on the mouth, before Toby stood to open the door. Sean patted his arse as he walked away. It was a gesture that said 'we aren't done yet,' and Toby hoped that was true.

Chapter Nine

Sadly, the arrival of the police and having to answer questions relating to the death of their neighbor did quell their passion, and Sean left shortly after the officers did, but not without hugging Toby and sharing another kiss. Toby watched Sean walk back to his flat and, on top of the usual feeling of desire, he felt a pang of affection. It frightened him that he was developing real feelings for someone so quickly, particularly a man who admitted he had never had a romantic connection with another man before. Was he heading for more heartache? And even if he was, was he really able to put a halt to things?

Toby lay awake for several hours that night, his head spinning with everything that had happened — Susan's death, the sight of her crushed head and crumpled body, his suspicions about Albert and, of course, the passionate kiss with Sean. Although he knew the kiss had happened, it seemed almost unreal, like a wonderful moment that someone else had experienced.

When Toby awoke in the early hours of the morning, he did so with a gasp, as if something had jolted him from sleep rather than it happening naturally. He lay listening to the near silence in the room. Then someone sniffed. There was a scuffing sound, as if someone or something was dragging itself across the carpet.

Toby was momentarily paralyzed with fear. *Someone is in my bedroom.* Now he could hear their rasping breaths as they crawled closer to the bed, and what sounded like the squelch of wet material. The noises seemed to fill the room, coming from all directions, making it impossible to pinpoint where the intruder was.

"Who's there?" he called, wrenching himself from the state of paralysis and fumbling for the bedside lamp switch. A brief vision of Albert crouched by his bed, drool dripping from his chin, flashed into Toby's mind. He found the switch and the room was doused in light. He looked around, first without moving from the bed, then finding the courage to push back the covers and stand. He opened the doors of the built-in wardrobe and even crouched down to look under the bed. *Nothing.*

He searched the rest of the flat, switching on lights as he went. There were no intruders and no feeling that there ever had been. He checked the front door and saw that the chain was on. He must have still been dreaming. It wasn't surprising after the night he'd had.

He returned to his bed and lay there, thinking of Sean just a few yards away in his own flat. He grew hard at the memory of their kiss and the feel of Sean's thick, solid cock. Toby slipped off his briefs and masturbated as he relived the experience. There was no need to invent stuff now. The reality of a kiss and his hand on that inviting bulge was enough to bring on an orgasm within seconds. As cum spattered across his stomach, Toby caught a movement out of the corner of his eye. He turned and saw her standing across the room next to the window. It was the woman, once again dressed in funeral garb, and she was grinning. But it was a dead grin, fixed and rotten, the teeth black, blood-rimmed and stained with earth. Her bone-white face was surrounded by a bush of flaming red hair.

Toby screamed.

But the scream did not break the hideous spell. She was still there, pointing an accusing finger, the long nail black with mud.

"Get out!" Toby yelled, and finally she backed away, fading through the wall. For a brief moment, he saw a transparent image of her floating outside the window, then she was gone.

Jesus!

Toby sat up, clutching his chest, trying to calm his pounding heart and his shaking hands. Now he knew why the rent was so low. Darkwater House was haunted.

* * * *

Toby didn't bother trying to sleep for the rest of the night. When he had calmed down, he got up and made himself a pot of coffee and sat at the breakfast bar in the kitchen drinking it, dry cum forming a crust on his stomach. For some reason, the kitchen seemed like the safest room.

He couldn't stay here, not with that thing prowling the house. But how could he leave? Where else would he get so much for so little? And there was the matter of Sean, his gorgeous neighbor, who was making it very obvious he wanted a sexual relationship — even if it was *just* sex he was after. If he moved out now, before anything had really developed, any interest Sean had would quickly fade.

Toby wondered if he was the only tenant to have seen the apparition. Had Susan been haunted by it too? Was that what had driven her to suicide? He had a sudden flashback of a girl standing at the end of his bed when he was around six years old, Toby screaming for his mother, being told he was dreaming but knowing he wasn't. That same little girl had returned several times for the two years they had lived in that house and Toby had eventually accepted her and learned not to mention her to anyone else. He'd almost forgotten about her.

As soon as it was light, he was going to knock on Sean's door, tell him what he'd seen and find out whether his neighbor had witnessed anything similar during his time at Darkwater House.

But by the time daylight arrived, Toby had persuaded himself not to confide in Sean. They'd only just gotten to know each other. How would Toby have felt if a man he'd only shared a kiss with turned up on his doorstep ranting about ghostly women in black appearing in his bedroom?

Could it have been a dream? Toby asked himself. He had seen his first dead body that evening. And with daylight now flooding the entire apartment and the heath in all its autumnal glory spread out like a great landscape painting beyond the many windows, Toby decided it could have been.

Even so, he decided to pay Albert a visit and do some prying. If there was a ghost in a house that had only been built in the sixties, the old man might know who it was and what it wanted.

But when he knocked on Albert's door a few hours later, he began to feel foolish. How could he bring up the subject of a ghost? The old man would think he was mad. When Albert didn't respond to his knock immediately, Toby felt relieved and took a step backward, ready to return to his flat and forget about investigating any hauntings. But then the door opened and Albert's expectant face appeared.

"Oh, hello," he greeted, opening the door wider. He was wearing a bathrobe and his scant, black hair was wet and clinging to his white scalp.

"I'm sorry," said Toby, retreating another step. "I've come at a bad time."

"Not at all," said Albert. "Come in. I've just put the kettle on."

Before Toby could protest, Albert was scurrying along the corridor, taking a right-hand turn into what Toby assumed was the kitchen. With a sigh, he followed Albert's damp footprints to the door through which he'd disappeared. In fact, it wasn't the kitchen but the living room and Albert was standing over a large, low coffee table, pouring tea from an elegant teapot into two cups. Where he was bending so low, his robe had risen up, revealing the bottom half of his buttocks, which were white and smooth, not the wrinkled prunes Toby would have imagined.

Why does he have a pot of tea and two cups ready? Toby wondered.

"Have a seat," said Albert, gesturing to a mustard-colored sofa, the minimalist design of which perfectly complemented the sixties architecture of Darkwater House. Indeed, all the furniture in Albert's living room had a sixties look to it. Toby was impressed by how cool his elderly neighbor's taste was. Maybe everything was a relic from when the house had first been built. Perhaps it wasn't that Albert had good taste. Maybe he just hadn't ever replaced any of the furniture since inheriting the house from his mother.

Toby took a seat and Albert sat in a sleek armchair opposite him. He opened his legs, offering an unwanted view up his robe. Toby made a point of not looking, praying that his landlord wouldn't try to seduce him.

Up close, the sofa was obviously an antique. The material was threadbare in places and there was a spring digging into Toby's arse — another reason to make this a brief visit.

"Milk and sugar?" asked Albert, leaning forward, milk jug poised over the cup nearest to Toby. The tea was bronze-colored and clearly stewed.

"Yes, please," said Toby, wondering how he could introduce the subject of the phantom woman.

From somewhere in the flat, Toby heard the sound of a mobile phone.

"Do you need to get that?" he asked, although the ringtone had already ceased.

"Get what?" asked Albert, pouring milk into his own cup.

"Your mobile phone was ringing," said Toby.

"I don't have one," said Albert, sitting back in his chair, cup and saucer resting on one bare knee.

Toby shrugged and took a sip of tea. It tasted like it looked, so over-brewed that it left a coating on his tongue. It was an effort not to grimace.

"So, is this just a social call?" asked Albert.

"Yes," said Toby, now thinking how weird that would look. It would possibly even give Albert the impression that Toby was interested in him. He needed to offer some explanation for his visit. "Plus, I had a few questions."

"Really?" Albert's grin was somehow both inviting and hostile.

"Oh, nothing serious," said Toby, unnerved by his host. "I'm just curious about the house and its history."

Albert didn't say anything, just sat, head cocked slightly to one side, waiting, like a bird of prey.

"Do you know when Darkwater House was built?" asked Toby.

"In the mid-sixties," said Albert. "My father was an architect. He designed it. It was a passion project. There was a derelict Victorian property on the grounds which had to be demolished, but within two years, Darkwater House was complete. It wasn't built as flats. He designed it as our family home. I would have been around six years old when we moved in. I can hardly remember where we lived before. It was a terrace house in Belsize Park that's probably worth a fortune now. This was supposed to be my parents' dream home, but it never really worked out like that."

"Why?" asked Toby, genuinely interested.

"It was all fine for a few years. Then my mother had another child and suffered from post-natal depression. It was all too much for my father and he left us. Within a year, he was living with a twenty-year-old trainee from his company. Mother was devastated, as you can imagine. She never recovered."

"That's sad," said Toby.

"It was indeed," agreed Albert. "At least my father did the right thing by her and gave her this house without taking it through the courts. Although, in retrospect, maybe she would have been better making a fresh start somewhere. Maybe we all would."

"Last night was terrible, wasn't it," said Toby. "Poor Susan. I met her. She was nice. I can't believe she did that. Is she the first tragedy the house has witnessed?"

"You make it sound as if the house is alive," said Albert.

Again, Toby was filled with a sense of unease.

"I just wondered," he said, "if there'd been any other deaths here, not that it matters."

"I'm sure it matters to the people left behind," said Albert.

"I didn't mean it like that," said Toby. "I just meant that it didn't affect how I felt about the house. I'm very happy here."

"That's good," said Albert. "I see you have made a friend, too."

Toby shifted his position, trying to edge his backside off the errant spring.

"You mean Sean?" he asked. "Yes, we went for a walk yesterday. He's okay, once you get past the brusque exterior."

"You seemed very close last night too," said Albert, "when you were upset over the body. I never saw him as the affectionate type."

Toby wasn't sure how to respond, but Albert hadn't finished yet.

"Be careful of him," he said.

"What?" Toby was too shocked by this sudden warning to form a complete sentence.

"He's a player," continued Albert. "He tried it on with me when he first moved in."

Toby laughed.

"I guess that seems funny to you," said Albert. "But men like him don't care about age or what someone looks like. He thinks he can use his youth and his looks to get whatever he wants. I know I told you not to bother trying to romance him, because he was straight, but I said that to protect you. I don't know if he's straight, gay or what, but he's happy to sleep with whoever he thinks is useful. That's the impression I get, anyway. How else would you explain him opening his door to me in a pair of briefs?"

Toby laughed again. "I don't think that means he was trying it on..." he began.

"Within five minutes of me entering his flat, he had my hand pressed to his bulge, offering me sex in exchange for waiving his first month's rent," said Albert. "And he was as hard as a rock, let me tell you."

Toby felt nauseous. He was sure this couldn't be true, but even the merest possibility that it could be was sickening.

"What did you do?" Toby asked, curious how far Albert would take the lie, despite his churning stomach.

Albert flushed and looked down into his teacup. "I'm embarrassed to admit that I almost accepted. I went as far as dropping to my knees and taking that monster of a cock into my mouth. He grabbed my head and started to push himself in and out, but then I regained some sense of propriety and left, but not before telling him that his rent was still the sum we had agreed to and that if he didn't like it, he could leave."

Toby stood and walked over the a nearby sideboard—another 1960s throwback made from a light-colored wood. Several framed photographs were arranged along its surface. Toby had only feigned interest in order to put some distance between Albert and his ridiculous lies, but one of the photos made him take a sharp breath. He picked it up and stared at the woman in the picture. She wearing a colorful maxi dress, standing outside a newer version of Darkwater House. Her voluminous hair was a vibrant red.

"Is this your mother?" he asked Albert.

Albert looked in his direction and nodded. "It was taken in the early seventies."

"She was very pretty," said Toby, although the version of her that he had met hadn't been pretty. He was certain that the woman in the image was the phantom who had tormented him the previous night and the night Sean had hit him. There was no mistaking that red hair.

He replaced the photo on the sideboard and turned back to face Albert.

"When did you lose her?" he asked.

"Around ten years ago," said Albert, obviously uncomfortable with the turn in the conversation. "You don't seem too bothered by what I just told you about Sean."

Toby shrugged. "It's none of my business," he said. "I hardly know him."

"Well, if you have any sense, you'll keep it that way," said Albert.

Toby was distracted by the same ringing tone he had heard before. This time, Albert obviously heard it too, although he ignored it.

"I'd better get on," he said. "I don't mean to be unsociable, but I am seeing my friend in Edgware again and I need to get dressed."

"Not at all," said Toby. "Thanks for the tea."

Albert showed him to the door. Toby was glad to be out of his flat. He felt tension lift as he made his way to the main front door. He needed some fresh air. Sean was jogging up the front drive as Toby stepped out.

"Hey there," Sean greeted.

"Your leg's better then," said Toby, holding the door open for him.

"Getting there," said Sean, maintaining eye contact. "You fancy doing something later?"

Toby hesitated. "I can't tonight," he said. "I'm seeing a friend."

"Shame," said Sean with a wink, as he slipped past Toby into the hall.

Toby caught a whiff of fresh, musky sweat and immediately regretted his decision. But there was a part of him that couldn't completely dismiss Albert's story. Plus, he needed time to think about the fact that he was apparently being haunted by the old man's dead mother.

Darkwater House was seeming less and less like a dream home.

Chapter Ten

After walking for around an hour, Toby spent the rest of the day emailing contacts, trying to drum up some work. He was relieved when two editors came back to him with a couple of feature commissions. Neither were too taxing and the deadline for each was two weeks away. He was worried about being able to focus on work with everything that was going on, but haunted or not, he still needed to pay the rent on his flat.

As evening approached, he remembered the lie he had told Sean about seeing a friend. All he wanted now was to be snuggled up next to his neighbor, watching a movie or just chatting. The more he considered Albert's story about Sean offering him sex in lieu of rent, the more ludicrous it sounded. Even in the short time he'd known Sean, Toby was sure he wasn't that kind of person. Albert, on the other hand, was a sad, lonely old man, with nothing better to do than fantasize about his tenants. Perhaps he even believed what he'd said was true.

Toby poured himself a glass of red wine—he'd bought a bottle while out walking—and tried watching TV. But there was nothing on but quiz shows and soaps, none of which interested him—and all he could think about was Sean. He wanted to feel that thick cock again, take it in his hand this time and jerk it until Sean came, his sexy face twisted with the pleasure of orgasm.

Just the thought of being with Sean had made Toby rock hard. He rubbed himself through his jeans, but fantasy wasn't enough. He wanted the real thing. He'd just tell Sean his plans had fallen through. Why sit here alone masturbating when his dream man was sitting across the corridor?

Toby waited for erection to subside—turning up at Sean's apartment with a boner might be just a bit too blatant—then headed to his front door. He turned the latch and pulled. The door wouldn't budge.

What the fuck?

Toby tried again, yanking more aggressively this time, but the door remained firmly closed. He checked to make sure he hadn't double-locked it with the chub key, then tried again. Still, no joy.

Without warning, a sense of utter dread washed over him, along with the sudden realization that someone or something was standing on the other side of the door. He was torn between backing away and peering through the peephole. If he looked, he would probably just see an empty corridor and he'd be able to laugh at his over-active imagination. He edged closer to the door, his heart pounding. He leaned forward, resting his eye against the peephole. She was standing just inches from the door, her haggard, earth-encrusted face looming into his line of vision, her eyes blazing with fury and her rigid grin revealing her blackened teeth. All was grays and black, apart from her flame red hair.

Toby yelled in shock and fear and stumbled backward. He swooned, gripping hold of the nearest piece of furniture—a bookcase—in a bid to stay upright. But the room spun and his head was filled with darkness.

When he came around, Toby instantly knew the phantom woman had gone. He felt disoriented, but the feeling of dread had evaporated. He sat up, groaning at the pain in his head, and pulled himself up, using the back of the sofa for support. He stumbled into the hallway and tried the front door. It opened easily, revealing the empty corridor beyond.

Toby breathed a sigh of relief, closed the door and returned to the living room. His head was throbbing. He sat on the sofa and downed the remnants of the red wine. His hand was shaking so that the wine sloshed around the glass.

He couldn't stay here, not with that creature stalking him, but what choice did he have? He'd signed a six-month contract. He could hardly cite 'haunting by landlord's dead mother' as grounds for breaking a legal agreement. Plus, there was Sean. Was he really prepared to give up living so close to a man he thought about almost constantly?

The vision of the dead woman's ghastly face filled his head, and Toby wasn't sure that even Sean was enough of a draw to keep him here. If he was going to stay, he needed to get to the bottom of why Albert's mother was haunting Darkwater House and lay her spirit to rest.

He didn't want to be alone, but if he went to Sean in this state, babbling about dead mothers, that really would end any chance of a relationship developing.

Toby took several more long, deep breaths. Eventually his heartbeat slowed and the trembling stopped. He looked at himself in the mirror above the fireplace, checking that the fear he felt wasn't too obvious in his eyes, then headed for Sean's apartment.

When Sean opened his door, Toby had to stifle a cry of pleasure. His neighbor was dressed in a short white bathrobe, his chest and its layer of dark hair exposed and his muscular legs perfectly displayed. The robe only fell to a few inches above the knee, so there was also the tantalizing knowledge that just above the hem hung Sean's cock and balls.

"Sorry to disturb you," said Toby. "I'm not seeing that friend after all and wondered if you were still free."

Sean smiled, his dark eyes shining. "I was just about to have a bath," he said. "I thought it might be good for my pulled muscle. Jogging today was a mistake. It's throbbing tonight."

"I'll leave you to relax then," said Toby, imagining something else throbbing beneath that robe.

"No, come in," said Sean, stepping to one side. "As long as you don't mind me having a soak while we chat, grab a beer from the fridge and come sit in the bathroom for a bit."

"Are you sure?" Toby's voice sounded annoyingly shrill all of a sudden.

Sean took him by the arm and pulled him into his apartment. "Give me a minute to get under the bubbles," he said, closing the front door and walking down the hallway to the bathroom. "Bring me a beer too."

Toby watched Sean walk away, admiring his broad shoulders and the way the robe pinched in at the waist and curved around his butt.

Sean looked back. "I'm dying of thirst here," he called, disappearing through the bathroom door.

Blushing, Toby hurried to find two beers, then, with a bottle in each hand, he headed to the bathroom. His heart was pounding almost as hard as when he'd seen the apparition through his spyhole. He hoped the sight of Sean naked in the bath wouldn't cause him to faint like that shock had.

Sean was immersed in bubbles. Only his head poked above the foam cover, then a hand and arm as he reached for his beer.

"Cheers," he said, hoisting himself into a sitting position, revealing his chest, the hair glistening with bubbles.

"Cheers," returned Toby, sitting on the closed lid of the toilet and taking a swig of beer.

"So, your friend let you down," said Sean.

"What?" Toby had momentarily forgotten his earlier lie. "Oh yes. I can't say I'm that disappointed."

Sean placed his beer bottle next to a row of shampoos and oils on a shelf on the wall next to the bath and began to lather up a bar of soap between his hands. Toby tried not to stare too hard as his neighbor soaped up his chest and arms, momentarily covering the vein-laced muscles in a sheen of white before splashing himself with water to rinse off. As his hands delved into the water, the bubbles were dispersed, offering Toby a short but heart-stopping glimpse of Sean's cock and balls. Even flaccid, his shaft was a good six inches, the bell-end blooming from a roll of foreskin.

It was all Toby could do not to release a despondent sigh when bubbles reformed over the perfect dick.

"Have you heard any more about the woman who jumped?" asked Sean, now washing his left thigh, lifting it out of the water and caressing it with his soapy hands.

"No," spluttered Toby. He was rock hard and the tight jeans he wore couldn't hide the fact. He rested his hands in his lap in a bid to cover the bulge, but that just drew Sean's attention to it.

"I wonder what made her do something like that," Sean continued, looking directly at Toby's full crotch. "I mean, sure we all get down. God knows, I've felt like shit for the past few months, but I wouldn't top myself over it."

Toby was trying to form a response, but he was totally distracted by Sean, who was now soaping up his crotch, tugging at his cock in order to give it a thorough cleaning. He wasn't attempting to hide it beneath the bubbles now. Toby wondered if Sean realized the effect he was having and was enjoying it. *Why else invite me into the bathroom?* Next, he'd be asking Toby to wash his back.

"Pass me that big towel, would you?" asked Sean, and with a grunt, he hoisted himself into a standing position. Water ran down his body, dripping from the end of his cock. His ballsac was still covered in bubbles.

Feeling slightly dizzy, Toby reached for the towel, which was hung over a heated rail, and passed it to Sean.

"Thanks, mate." Sean chose to dry his hair first, the efforts causing his cock and balls to jiggle, shaft bouncing against one firm thigh.

"Fuck me," whispered Toby, massaging his own cock through his jeans while Sean's face was covered by the towel.

"What's that?" asked Sean, now stepping out of the bath and bending to dry his legs. Toby wished he was sitting behind Sean, so that he could see those arse cheeks parting as he bent.

"Nothing," murmured Toby. "To be honest, I'm finding this a bit of a turn-on."

Sean stood upright. "That was the general idea," he said with a grin. "Now, will you get on your knees and suck this feller?" He threw the towel on the floor and grabbed his cock, pulling the foreskin right back so that glans visibly swelled.

"Fuck yes!" said Toby, already kneeling in front of Sean and nuzzling his damp balls before taking his cock into his mouth. It tasted of clean bathwater and pre-cum. He took it down his throat so that his lips brushed against Sean's pubic hair. By the time he pulled back, Sean was hard and groaning appreciatively. Toby teased the swollen glans of Sean's cock with his tongue, tracing each curve and dip. Sean's moaning grew louder, and he rested a hand on Toby's head, thrusting his hips backward and forward, so that his cock slid in and out of Toby's mouth. When Toby pulled back to take a breath, a long string of pre-cum stretched from Sean's cock to his bottom lip. His leaned in and slurped the delicious salty liquid into his mouth, feeling it melt onto his tongue.

Sean pulled Toby to his feet and kissed him passionately on the mouth. His breath was minty, as if he'd been expecting this, although there was no way he could have been.

"Shall we go to the bedroom?" he asked.

Toby nodded and allowed himself to be led from the bathroom down the narrow hallway.

In the bedroom, Sean undressed him, pulling his T-shirt over his head and discarding it on the floor then slowly unbuttoning his fly, delving his hand into the resulting gap and massaging Toby's aching cock through his briefs. He punctuated each stage of the undressing process with a kiss, first on the lips then on Toby's neck, working down to his chest, nibbling each nipple before planting a gentle kiss on each of them, making them tingle.

Sean crouched in order to pull down Toby's jeans and briefs. Toby had already kicked off his trainers and socks, and soon he had stepped out of his remaining clothes, so that he stood completely naked before Sean. Sean stood gradually, kissing Toby's cock, stomach and chest on his way up, ending with another forceful kiss on the mouth.

"I really want to fuck you," he said, his Irish accent made stronger by lust.

"Yes," breathed Toby, gripping Sean's arse in both hands and pulling him close so that their cocks rubbed together, their pre-cum mingling, its aroma rising.

"Please tell me you have condoms," said Toby, falling back onto the bed and pulling Sean with him.

"I do," said Sean, reaching into a draw in the bedside table. "I bought them today while I was out running."

"So, you had this planned, did you?" asked Toby, as Sean slipped the sheath over his cock and smeared it with a generous dollop of lube.

"Not at all," said Sean, now kneeling between Toby's legs, which he lifted and draped over his shoulders. He smeared Toby's hole with lube, sliding a finger inside him for an instant. Toby groaned at the wonderful combination of pain and pleasure.

As Sean edged his cock inside his arse, Toby stared up into his stunning brown eyes, remembering how, not so long ago, they had looked back at him with disdain. Now they simmered with desire. Toby looped an arm around Sean's shoulders and pulled him down for a kiss, crying out as the man's long, thick cock filled him.

Chapter Eleven

When Toby woke the next morning, the brief moment of disorientation was followed by a feeling of warmth and contentment. He was in Sean's bed, and last night they had made love for hours before falling asleep. Toby rolled over to look at his lover, but Sean's side of the bed was empty. *Maybe he's making us coffee?*

Toby didn't bother to dress. The time for modesty was long past. He wandered naked along the passageway until he reached the kitchen. Sean was sitting at the breakfast bar, fully clothed and drinking coffee. He glanced up as Toby entered but quickly looked away again.

"Morning," greeted Toby. He had thought about kissing Sean on the cheek, but there was an unexpected chill in the atmosphere.

"Hi," said Sean, draining his mug and standing. "I need to go. I'm meeting a friend who may have work for me next week. You can see yourself out, right?"

"Err-r, sure," said Toby, now wishing he had dressed before venturing from the bedroom. If there was one thing worse than being rejected, it was being rejected while naked. "Is everything okay?"

"Fine," said Sean. "I'm just running late."

Toby stepped aside to allow Sean to pass.

"Do me a favor and stick the sheets in the washing machine before you go," said Sean as he opened the front door.

Toby felt as if he'd been punched in the gut. He waited for the door to close behind Sean, then let out a sob. He wiped the tears from his face and stomped through to the bedroom, yanking the sheets from the bed and bundling them up into a ball.

"Fuck this," he snapped, throwing the bedding onto the floor. "Do your own washing."

He dressed, remembering how Sean had removed each item the night before, and more tears streamed down his face. What the hell had happened between them falling asleep and this morning?

By the time he was back in his own flat, he was depressed rather than angry. Obviously, Sean had been drunk the night before, even though he hadn't seemed it, and when he'd woken up and seen Toby lying next to him, he'd instantly regretted what had happened.

But it was Sean who had pushed things forward. He'd initiated the kissing the previous day. If the police hadn't turned up, they would no doubt have ended up in bed then. His sudden mood change made no sense. Toby felt angry again.

He needed to get out and walk off his bad mood. He could start working on the features he'd been commissioned to write later. He wouldn't be able to concentrate while he felt like this, anyway.

He grabbed his coat and flung open the front door. Sean was standing outside his own apartment and there was a woman with him — a tall, attractive blonde woman. Toby froze, staring at them. Sean glanced in his direction, then continued to unlock the door to his flat, ushering the woman before him. He looked back at Toby for an instant, his expression unreadable, then followed his guest, closing the door behind him.

* * * *

While the heath was its usual beautiful self, it didn't have its normal restorative effect on Toby. He wandered aimlessly along the various paths and muddy walkways, sometimes getting completely lost, before emerging onto a path that seemed familiar and eventually finding his way to a known landmark, such as the duck pond or the bandstand, where today, a group of people were holding a birthday party. Toby stood glaring at the happy bunch, the colorful balloons and screaming children running in circles around their Champagne-supping parents. *What do they have to be so jolly about? And when will it be my turn to be happy? Will I ever meet a nice, decent guy I can share my life with?*

He walked on, vaguely heading toward Darkwater House, although he always lost all sense of direction over the heath. It was so vast and its terrain so varied.

His mood hadn't vastly improved by the time he arrived back at the house. It plummeted even further when he discovered Albert loitering in the communal hallway. He was pretending to dust around the door frame, but Toby couldn't smell any polish.

"Ah, Toby, perfect timing," he said, fixing Toby with his watery gaze. "We have a little problem."

"What kind of problem?" asked Toby.

"We'd better chat in my flat," said Albert, already leading the way. With a sigh, Toby followed.

"I checked my bank account this morning and I noticed your first month's rent is short," said Albert, once he had closed his front door. He didn't suggest they go through to the living room.

"What? No, that can't be right," protested Toby. "I transferred eight hundred pounds on the day I moved in. It definitely left my account."

"Eight hundred?" said Albert.

"Yes, that's what we agreed on," said Toby.

Albert laughed. "I'm a generous man, Toby, but are you seriously suggesting I would rent a flat of that size with a view of Hampstead Heath for eight hundred pounds a month?"

Toby was too flabbergasted to form a reply.

"We agreed on one thousand five hundred a month, which is a fraction of what you would normally pay for a property like this."

"Albert, you know that's not true," said Toby, frustration and confusion making him tearful. He couldn't deal with this, not today.

"It's all in the lease that you signed," said Albert, waving several stapled pieces of paper under Toby's nose. "See? Right here in black and white."

Toby snatched the contract from Albert and scanned it until he reached the part about rent. It clearly stated one thousand five hundred pounds. Toby remembered signing it in this very flat a few days earlier. He also recalled how little attention he had paid to the content.

"You tricked me into signing this," he said. "Or you've changed it. I can't afford this amount. You know I can't."

"Oh dear," said Albert. "That puts me in a rather embarrassing position. I can't let you stay when you owe me so much money."

"Why are you doing this?" demanded Toby, resisting the urge to throttle the old man and shove the lease down his throat.

Albert sighed and took the paperwork back, poring over it thoughtfully.

"Perhaps we could come to some agreement," he said. "Something a little like the one you suggested when you came to look at the flat."

"I didn't suggest anything," insisted Toby. "I wanted to make it clear that I wasn't up for any quid-pro-quo agreement like that."

"Still, you put the idea into my head, and now that I've had time to think about it, it doesn't seem like such a bad idea. I can bring the rent down to a more affordable one thousand pounds a month, in return for a few favors from yourself. Shall we say one visit per week?"

"You can say it, but it won't be happening!" stormed Toby.

"I don't expect sex," said Albert, face flushing, "just a performance."

"Like a song and dance routine," said Toby with a bitter laugh.

"I was thinking something more...naked," said Albert. "I think I'd enjoy watching you pleasure yourself. I wouldn't even touch you. You could just perch your sweet bottom on my coffee table and jerk yourself off while I sit and watch with a cup of tea. It would be quite civilized, really, and you'd get to keep your lovely flat and continue living by the equally lovely Sean. Did you have fun last night, by the way?"

"Mind your own business!" snapped Toby. "And you can shove that lease up your arse. If you want me out, you'll have to throw me out."

"And I will," said Albert. "Well, I won't personally throw you out, but I do have some very helpful associates who are always happy to discard any unwanted tenants for me. Big brutes, they are, and very clumsy with people and their possessions."

Toby wrenched open the front door and ran for the stairs. He was sobbing when he reached his flat, and from somewhere in the house, he was sure he could hear laughter.

* * * *

When he eventually calmed down, Toby found his copy of the rental agreement and confirmed that it did indeed state that the monthly rent would be one thousand five hundred pounds. *How could I have been so stupid? Is this how Albert operates? Tricking young guys into signing leases then forcing them into a perverse sexual relationship?* That made no sense. Susan hardly fit that scenario and she'd said how cheap her rent was. None of the other tenants he'd seen, apart from Sean, fit the description either. So why was he picking on Toby? Was it jealousy over his relationship with Sean? Was it possible that he could have snuck into his flat while he was at Sean's and replaced the real lease with this one? It would be simple enough to replace the page that stated the rent with a fresh one. Toby had only signed the last page of three.

Toby poured himself a large glass of red wine from one of the bottles he had bought shortly after the confrontation with Albert and carried it through to the living room. He stood by one of the windows staring out at the heath, watching it fade into darkness as dusk fell. Maybe he should take this as a sign. He'd been thinking of leaving anyway. The place was haunted by Albert's mad, dead mother, for Christ's sake. Why would he stay?

But where would he go at such short notice? He didn't have enough money to pay a month in advance and a deposit on anther flat, and he still hadn't built bridges with any of his old friends, certainly not enough to ask if he could stay with them for months. He might just be able to scrape together enough money to pay Albert the rest of this month's rent, but after that, he'd either have to leave or give in to the old pervert's demands.

By the time he'd finished the first bottle of wine, the idea of performing for Albert seemed less repellent. He might even get a weird kick out of it. He'd wanked off on web cam sites before now and had all kinds of people watch him, including old men.

When he'd drank another glass from the second bottle, the scenario was seeming quite appealing.

He walked to the lift in an alcoholic fog, actually aroused at the thought of what he was about to do.

Even when Albert opened the door to his flat and offered his insipid smile, Toby wasn't deterred.

"Okay," he said. "I'll do it. But only once a month. And the rent has to be eight hundred as we originally agreed."

Albert considered this for a moment, then offered Toby his hand. "Agreed," he said.

"Do you want to start now?" asked Toby

"I'm free if you are," said Albert. "Why don't you come through to the living room?"

"Do you have anything to drink?" asked Toby, following him. He didn't want to sober up midway through his performance.

While Albert fixed them both drinks, Toby surveyed the photographs on the sideboard once again. This time he was drawn to one of a handsome young man, sitting on a bench, possibly on Hampstead Heath. He looked like he was in his early twenties and was dressed in timeless fashion—a white shirt and a gray blazer. His hair was almost black and he had bright green eyes that stared straight into the camera.

Albert was suddenly behind him, holding out a glass of gin and tonic. "I was a handsome devil, wasn't I," he said with a sigh.

"This is you?" asked Toby, not trying to hide his surprise.

"Yes," said Albert, placing a hand on the small of Toby's back. "But what say you stop admiring old pictures of me, and let me do some admiring of you."

"How do you want to do this?" asked Toby, taking a gulp of his drink.

"I'll sit here," said Albert, planting himself on the couch. "And you stand over there on the other side of the coffee table. And when you're ready, start undressing...slowly. I want to savor every second. When you're nice and naked, I will give you instructions. Nothing too kinky, all good clean fun."

"Nothing about this feels clean or fun," said Toby, taking up his position. Although part of him was turned on by the sordid nature of the situation—the idea that he was going to bring so much pleasure to someone simply by masturbating in front of them. It couldn't feel any worse than being rejected by Sean after making love with him all night.

"Whenever you're ready," said Albert.

Toby closed his eyes and began to lift his T-shirt over his head. If he didn't look at Albert, maybe he could get through this without throwing up.

He chucked the T-shirt onto the nearest chair and caressed his chest with both hands, staring at the ceiling, anywhere but at Albert. With one hand he unbuttoned the fly of his jeans then pushed them down to his knees. He could hear Albert's breathing growing louder and faster. He hoped the man wasn't masturbating. He reached for his drink, which he'd placed on the coffee table, and downed the rest of it in one hit before massaging his cock through his white briefs, trying to get it hard. No doubt that was what Albert would expect for his money. He imagined it was the young Albert from the photograph sitting opposite him, watching him with inquisitive eyes — and that helped. He began to grow hard and pushed the hem of his briefs lower, allowing his cockhead to bloom above it.

I'm doing this so I don't end up homeless, he told himself.

He kicked off his shoes and stepped out of his jeans, so that he was dressed in just his socks and briefs. He was fully hard now, trying not to focus on Albert's ragged breathing, picturing the cute guy on the bench, reminding himself that the Albert in this room was that same person, just older. He pushed his briefs down to his thighs and began to masturbate — pushing his foreskin over his cockhead then pulling it back, so that his glans bloomed like an exotic bud.

"Lovely..." whispered the old man, and just the sound of his lust-filled voice was too much to bear.

"I can't," said Toby, grabbing his clothes from where he'd thrown them. "I thought I could do it, but I can't."

He dressed quickly, aware of Albert's protests.

When he finally looked at his landlord, the old man was obviously livid.

"We had an agreement," he said.

"I'll pay you the rest of this month's rent tomorrow," said Toby, pushing his feet back into his shoes. "And I'll be out by the end of the month."

"You signed a six-month contract," said Albert, rising from the sofa. "I could sue you for the whole amount."

"Do that!" snapped Toby. "And maybe I'll pay a visit to the police and tell them how my perverted landlord tried to blackmail me into having sex with him. How would you like a sexual abuse charge against you? Maybe I'll convince Sean to come with me and tell them how you groped him on his first day here. And how many other young guys have you tried this kind of thing with over the years? I bet I'm not the first. I'm a journalist, remember? I'm good at unearthing secrets."

"Get out!" shouted Albert. "And you'd better be out by the end of this month or I will have you thrown out. And if you ever threaten me again…"

Toby didn't hear the end of that sentence. He was already in the communal hallway and heading for the lift.

Chapter Twelve

Despite barely sleeping all night and feeling like death warmed up, Toby spent the following morning researching the features he'd been commissioned to write. One was a piece on the rise of the gastro pub for a publication read by those working in the restaurant industry, the other a column on the demise of the gay pub for an LGBTI website he had contributed to a few times in the past. As he worked, he kept glancing out of the nearest window and sighing at the gorgeous view. He'd known from the minute he'd stepped into this room that it was too good to be true. He hadn't foreseen just how bad it would all turn out — that Albert was a pervert and a con artist and that the house was haunted by his seemingly deranged mother.

Toby thought about what he'd said to Albert about being a journalist who was used to unearthing secrets. He'd made himself sound like some bigshot reporter, when the truth was that he mostly just wrote articles about pubs and restaurants, and they were usually only published in magazines hardly anyone read. There had been the one feature published by *The Times* — an article about the rise of veganism, just before it became such a massive trend — but that kind of success had never been repeated. Whatever his journalism credentials, however, he could still do some research into the Darkwater name. Sometimes a simple search online could unearth plenty.

He typed 'Darkwater House' into the search field, but the only results were for old properties in other parts of the country. Next, he typed in 'Darkwater, Mrs.' and 'obituary'. Again, nothing that came up related to the Mrs. Darkwater that he was interested in. He tried 'Mrs. Darkwater, Hampstead'. The fourth link down was to the archives of a local Hampstead newspaper. Toby clicked on it. The headline of the story was *Local Woman Missing After Swimming in Hampstead Ponds*. Toby scanned the text. That was her, Albert's mother.

The story related how Miriam Darkwater had last been seen by her son Albert, heading to the women's pond on Hampstead Heath. Despite being in her late seventies, Miriam was a regular at the pond, according to the story. When Miriam still hadn't returned home by early evening, Albert had walked over to the pond himself and asked those leaving the area if they had seen his mother. When he couldn't find her or any word of her, he reported her missing to the police. Toby clicked on a link to a later story, which reported that no body had been found in the pond, despite divers conducting a thorough search. Search teams had also scoured the heath, but no body had been discovered. The story was ten years old. Toby assumed that after the requisite seven years, Miriam Darkwater had been declared officially dead. But why hadn't Albert mentioned that his mother had gone missing? He'd talked as if she had died of old age. He certainly hadn't said anything to suggest a story of this nature. Was it possible she wasn't dead at all? Had Toby actually seen Miriam Darkwater in the flesh and just imagined the rest?

She floated above the ground and passed through a wall, he reminded himself.

He jumped at the sound of someone knocking on his front door. He hoped it wasn't Albert looking for another confrontation. He put his eye to the spy hole and saw Sean's handsome face. *This will be interesting.*

Toby opened the door, but not fully. He didn't want to seem too welcoming.

"Hi," said Sean. "I guess you know why I'm here."

"I've absolutely no idea," said Toby. "I'm actually working, so I can't chat."

"I just wanted to apologize about yesterday morning," said Sean, and his beautiful brown eyes were filled with what looked like genuine remorse. "I behaved like a total dick. I really enjoyed that night. It was great. But I did feel a bit strange when I woke up. I've never actually woken up with a guy before. It was a new sensation."

"I'm sorry I spoiled your morning," said Toby. "It must have been horrific for you, waking up to the sight of me lying next to you."

"No, it wasn't," said Sean. "That was just it. When I say it felt strange, I didn't mean in a bad way. It actually felt right. I loved that you were there. Then I freaked out a bit because I've never felt that way about a guy before. It's always just been about sex. But when I looked at you, I wanted to kiss you, then get up and make us coffee and go buy some newspapers to read while we drank it in bed. Couple stuff."

"You hid that well," said Toby.

"Like I said, I freaked out. I suddenly felt frightened — scared that I was falling for a guy and what that would mean. I tried to imagine coming out to my family and it made me feel sick. Then, to make things worse, my ex texted and asked to meet. That was the blonde woman you saw me with. She insisted on seeing where I was living. I was praying you wouldn't still be there. Can you imagine how awkward that would have been?"

"Well, I'm glad I didn't embarrass you," said Toby. "I felt just great, by the way. I love being fucked all night then made to feel like a leper the next morning. It got my day off to a brilliant start."

"I really am *so* sorry," said Sean.

"The good news is that you won't have to put up with me cramping your style much longer. Albert's nearly doubled my rent and told me to get out by the end of the month if I can't afford it."

"Are you serious?"

Toby nodded. "I could have stripped for him in lieu of a share of the rent, but I decided that was too low for even me to stoop. I thought about it, though, after two bottles of wine. I even went to his flat and started to remove my clothes. That's how great you made me feel about myself. I didn't go through with it. I decided I was worth more than that, no matter what some people might think of me."

Toby decided there was no need to reveal just how far he'd gone.

"Is there anything I can do to make up for the way I behaved?" asked Sean. "I'm serious. I feel terrible. I was such a dickhead. A total prat. I'm cringing inside just thinking about what a douchebag I was."

"Don't worry about it. I hope you and the blonde are very happy together."

Sean shook his head. "I'm not getting back with her," he said. "I told her I'd met someone else, as a matter of fact. I didn't say it was the fella across the hall."

Toby blushed. "Well, that wouldn't be true, would it," he said. "We're not seeing each other. You've made it clear that you're not into guys in that way. I totally get that. But there was no need to make me feel so used. I can cope with a 'friends with benefits' relationship, but there needs to be some kind of respect on your side."

"I've stopped freaking out now," said Sean, taking Toby's hand in his. "I mean, I'm still not ready to come out to my family or wear an 'I'm queer and I'm here' T-shirt to the next building site I work on, but I do want to see where this goes — that is, if I haven't pissed you off so much that you never want to see me again."

Toby wanted to fling the door open wide, wrap his arms around Sean and cover his face with kisses, but he managed to restrain himself.

"Why don't we go for a drink tonight," he suggested, "and see what happens?"

"Sounds like a plan," said Sean. "Thank you for not just telling me to fuck off. I would have done that. Oh, and I really am going to meet someone now about a possible job, so wish me luck."

"Good luck," said Toby, and he leaned forward and kissed Sean on the cheek. Sean smiled sheepishly and a blush spread across his face.

"Thanks," he said. "I'll knock for you about seven."

Toby watched him walk away and grinned. Maybe life wasn't so bad after all. Then he felt the familiar wave of anxiety, and the inner voice whispering about the danger of taking risks, of opening up to men like Sean. He took a lingering look at Sean's perfect butt before he turned the corner at the end of the corridor.

"I'll take that risk," he murmured.

* * * *

His mood dramatically lifted by the conversation with Sean, Toby made good progress with both features that day, finally closing his laptop at five in the evening and running a bath. He was going to take a leaf out of Sean's book and enjoy a nice, long soak before getting ready for his date. He shivered with excitement—both at the thought of going on an actual date with Sean and at the memory of him lying in his bath and the love-making that had followed. Having Sean inside him, those dark eyes staring into his, had, without a doubt, been the most erotic experience of Toby's life.

By the time Toby climbed into the bath, he was hard. He tugged on his cock a few times but refrained from having a full-on wank. He wanted to save himself for Sean, assuming they ended up in bed tonight. There was no guarantee the evening would develop that way. Maybe Sean would 'freak out' again and decide dating a guy just wasn't for him—that he was purely a quick-blow-job-in-the-bushes kind of man.

Toby managed to smile, despite partly fearing such a scenario.

The attack came without warning. One moment he was relaxing, the heat of the water lulling him into a pleasant doze, the next his face was under water and something was holding it there. He reached out with both hands, groping the air above him, but could see no one. Still, some force was keeping his head submerged and he desperately needed to breathe. He managed to grip the sides of the bath and tried to hoist himself up, but whatever was attacking him was stronger than he was. He wanted to scream but that would mean opening his mouth, which would be disastrous. He'd already swallowed too much water on his way under.

He hammered on the side of the bath. Maybe the noise would alert one of the neighbors. But by the time Albert would arrive with a spare set of keys, Toby would have drowned. Panic filled him. He was going to die. *This is it*. Through the surface of the bathwater he saw a face. It took him a second to recognize Albert. He looked different — younger. He wasn't as young as in the photograph on the sideboard but a good decade younger than he looked now. It was this version of Albert that was trying to drown him. Blackness began to creep across his vision. He was going to pass out. His attacker looked deranged, his face twisted with rage and hatred.

Then as suddenly as it had started, the attack stopped. Toby hauled himself upright with a choking gasp, spewing forth a jet of water. His eyes also streamed, and for a few moments, he couldn't see. When his vison cleared he scanned the room, his knuckles white where he still gripped the sides of the bath,

The door was locked and there was no one else in the bathroom.

Chapter Thirteen

"Are you okay" asked Sean, standing just inside Toby's flat.

Toby shook his head. He had dressed, ready to go out, but was too shaken by earlier events to act as if everything was fine. He was going to have to confide in Sean, even if it did make him look like a madman.

"What's up?" asked Sean, following Toby into the living room.

"You may leave as soon as I tell you this," said Toby, "but I have to share it with someone or I am going to go crazy — or maybe end up dead."

"Jesus," said Sean, perching on an arm of the sofa. "Go on."

"I think I'm being haunted by Albert's dead mother," said Toby, and waited for Sean to laugh.

"Thank God for that," he said. "I thought you might have changed your mind about going for a drink."

Toby stared at him. "Is that it?"

Sean shrugged. "I've felt something weird about this place since the second I stepped through the front gate.

I haven't seen anything, but I'm not surprised it's haunted. I assumed that was the reason it was so cheap. My childhood home in Ireland was haunted. I never saw that ghost either, but I used to hear her sometimes, crashing around in the kitchen. My mum saw her. She said she looked like a woman from the 1800s who was very angry, apparently."

"So, you don't think I'm mad?"

"Not yet," said Sean. "I may change my mind when you tell me the whole story, but shall we do that over a drink?"

"Definitely," said Toby, grabbing his coat from the back of the sofa. "Let's get out of here."

"Have you seen a ghost before?" asked Sean in the lift.

Toby nodded. "A few times when I was a kid, but not since I've been an adult. I thought I'd just imagined the other one, until now. Sean, I think something terrible happened to Albert's mother. After what just happened in my flat, I think Albert may have murdered her."

As they walked toward Hampstead High Street, Toby told Sean about his encounters with the ghost and the most recent incident in the bath.

"Jesus, that sounds terrifying," said Sean. "You know how much I enjoy a relaxing bath."

Toby couldn't help but smile. "It's not funny," he said. "I thought I was going to drown. But I don't think I was meant to die. I think it was the ghost trying to send a message, to let me know how she died."

Sean pushed open the door to an old-fashioned pub set at the top of a dramatically upward-sloping alleyway just off the main road. Toby couldn't remember even discussing where they would go, but he liked the idea of having a drink here. Warmth billowed from the bar, and the only noise was the low hum of chatter.

They ordered drinks and found a table in a private corner to one side of a cavernous fireplace.

"Are you definitely sure you didn't fall asleep in the bath and have a vivid dream?" asked Sean. "God knows, I've had a few nightmares about Albert."

Toby shook his head. "It didn't feel like a dream. It felt real...very real. Something was holding my head under the water, but they released me just before I would have needed to take a breath. They wanted me to live so that I could tell people what I'd seen — Albert holding someone under the water, drowning them."

"His mother?" Sean took a long sip of lager.

"Well, that would make sense. I've seen her a few times and she looked really pissed off, apart from when I saw her outside the house and when I was walking back over the heath. That version of her was totally different. She was dressed in normal clothes and she wasn't wailing or floating."

"Albert certainly fits the profile of a killer," said Sean. "He has psycho written all over him. I bet if we peered in through a window now, we'd see him dressed in one of his mother's frocks, holding a conversation with himself."

Toby frowned. "You're not taking this seriously, are you? Sometimes I miss serious, grumpy Sean."

"I am," Sean assured him. "But what can we do? We can hardly go to the police with the story you just told me, and I'm guessing Albert was never under suspicion if there was nothing online about it."

"There were only a couple of stories online," said Toby. "But that doesn't necessarily mean Albert wasn't investigated. Maybe the local press just lost interest in the story."

"So, all we know is that Albert told the police that the last time he saw his mother she was heading to the women's pond for a swim?" asked Sean.

Toby nodded.

"I tried swimming in the men's pond when I first moved in," said Sean. "That water is freezing. I thought my heart was going to stop. My cock shriveled to the size of a banana."

"But then wouldn't they have found her body?" asked Toby, making a point of not laughing at Sean's attempt at a joke.

"I don't know how deep that pond gets. Are there any other cases where someone was thought to have drowned there and no body was found?"

"Not sure," said Toby, taking a swig of red wine. "I'll check when I get back."

"Won't you be scared in your flat all alone?" asked Sean, raising his dark eyebrows.

"Are you asking me back to yours?" asked Toby.

"We could just spoon all night," said Sean. "I doubt Mrs. Darkwater will pay a visit while I'm there. I can't stay up half the night, though. I actually have a job to go to tomorrow."

"Really?" Toby felt guilty for not having asked how Sean's meeting had gone.

"Yep. My mate Ted has a big house renovation job on and he needs a skilled carpenter onboard. It should be a few weeks' work at least, and once he remembers how good I am, I bet there will be lots more work after this job ends."

"That's brilliant," said Toby, clinking his glass against Sean's. "Congratulations."

"Another drink?" asked Sean.

"Yeah, let's have another one, then maybe we can get down to some serious spooning," replied Toby.

Sean hesitated, half standing. "I'll be the big spoon, right, and you'll be the little spoon?"

Toby laughed. "Of course."

He watched Sean walk to the bar, still turned on by the sight of his tight butt in those clinging jeans. He couldn't quite believe he was sleeping with his gorgeous neighbor. It wasn't often that he fantasized about someone the way he had with Sean, and for it to turn into something real... It was a pity the thrill of this new relationship was being partly eclipsed by other events. He wanted to relax and enjoy a couple of drinks before curling up in bed with a man he fancied more than anyone he'd ever met. *Even Joe never turned me on like Sean does.*

When Sean returned with their drinks, Toby wanted to lean forward and kiss him, but he knew Sean wouldn't like that. He still wanted to keep up the straight-guy pretense in public.

"If you're serious about Albert being a killer, how do we go about proving it?" asked Sean, leaning back in his chair with a pensive expression.

"I guess finding his mother's remains would be a start. If she didn't really go to the pond that morning and he drowned her in the bath, what did he do with her body?"

"I think we'd be able to smell it if he'd stashed her somewhere in the house," said Sean. "Or the tenants living here back then would have."

"What about somewhere in the grounds or on the heath?" suggested Toby.

"Wouldn't a dog have sniffed her out if she was in a shallow grave on the heath?" suggested Sean.

"Which means it would be somewhere on the property," said Toby.

"What do you suggest? That we buy a couple of spades and start digging up the back garden?" asked Sean.

Toby tutted and took a gulp of wine. "You're still not taking this seriously."

"I am, I am," Sean assured him, sitting forward and fixing Toby with an earnest gaze, which made Toby want to kiss him again. "I just don't know what we can do with no real evidence except a vision you had while in the bath."

Toby sighed. "You're right," he said. "I'll just forget about it. I'll be moving out in a few weeks anyway. I just need to work out where to go."

"Don't say that," said Sean. "I like having you living close by."

"We could still see each other. I won't be moving to the other side of the world. I'll probably be sleeping in a doorway on Hampstead High Street."

"One thing we can do is prove Albert did something dodgy with your lease agreement," said Sean. "Mine is for eight hundred pounds per month and it's the same size as your flat, so if he's charging you more than that, he doesn't have a leg to stand on. We could speak to the other tenants. If we find out they're all paying less than you, we have an even stronger case. I'm sure just the threat of involving a solicitor would be enough for him to back down."

"That's true," said Toby. "But do I really want to live somewhere where the landlord and his dead mother seem to have it in for me?"

"Yes," said Sean, maintaining his serious expression. "When your neighbor is this hot, you do."

Toby laughed and allowed his knee to brush against Sean's under the table. Sean returned the pressure.

"Maybe we could have a bit of fun before we spoon," Sean whispered, leaning forward so that Toby felt his warm breath on his face.

Toby downed his wine in several gulps and replaced the glass on the table. "I'm ready to leave when you are," he said with a grin.

Despite the traumatic episode in the bath, Toby found himself laughing most of the way back to Darkwater House. A couple of times, Sean draped an arm around his shoulder and pulled him close, but he would quickly remember they were in public and his arm would drop back to his side after a few seconds. It still felt good, though.

As they turned the corner into their road, Toby froze.

"What's wrong?" asked Sean, grinding to a halt beside him.

Toby pointed toward Darkwater House. Standing by the gate and wearing a dark shawl that was blowing in the wind like great bat wings was the red-haired woman.

Chapter Fourteen

"It's her!" exclaimed Toby, pointing.

"Who?" Sean looked from Toby's stricken face to the flame-haired woman, who had yet to notice them.

"Mrs. Darkwater!" said Toby.

"But that's not a ghost," said Sean.

The woman suddenly glanced in their direction and, perhaps sensing their scrutiny, turned quickly and hastened toward the alleyway that ran down to the heath along the side of the house.

Without thinking, Toby bolted after her.

"Toby!" Sean yelled.

When Toby reached the end of the track, he saw the woman, who was now also running, disappear around the back of the house. He gave chase, aware of Sean still calling him and the sound of his feet clattering along the pavement. Mud spattered up Toby's legs as he ran, his feet squelching in the rain-sodden ground. Soon Sean was beside him.

"Are you sure about this?" he asked, placing a hand on Toby's shoulder as they slowed at the edge of the heath, Toby scanning the surrounding area for the woman.

"There!" he pointed. The woman was halfway down the slope leading to the meadow that Toby had walked across on his first day. She was almost invisible in the darkness, shrouded by her black cape.

"That is *not* a ghost," said Sean. "And she is definitely not a woman in her eighties either, not unless she has taken some serious performance-enhancing drugs."

"Come on!" said Toby, running and skidding down the slope.

The woman glanced over her shoulder. Toby could tell she was no phantom, but he needed to know who she was and why she had tried to run away. With that hair, she was surely related to Miriam Darkwater in some way.

"Please wait!" he called, but she was now pelting across the meadow, heading toward the main path that cut through the center of the heath.

In the darkness, Toby almost lost his footing several times. The blackness became so dense after a few minutes of heading away from the house that Toby stopped and considered giving up. He couldn't even see the woman anymore. Sean caught up with him again, this time grabbing his arm.

"Toby, come on, man. This is going too far. She looked frightened. You can't just chase after strange women in the dark."

"But what if she knows something?"

"What? Because she has red hair?" asked Sean.

"She looks like Miriam Darkwater. Why was she hanging around the gate? And I think I saw her when I first moved in, loitering at the back of the house."

"She was probably here to see Albert and we just scared the shit out of her," said Sean.

"Let's just see if we can find her and explain," begged Toby. "Just come with me a bit farther. If there's no sign of her, we'll go home."

"Okay," relented Sean. "But if she reports us for harassment or something, I'm throwing you under a bus."

"Good to know," said Toby, jogging, rather than running, on. Sean sighed and kept pace with him.

Being on the main part of the heath after dark made Toby feel like a trespasser. It was a different feeling from venturing into the gay cruising area. Even though the action that took place there was illegal, it had felt less clandestine than this adventure. It was like exploring an alternative world, where things were familiar but not the same. They reached the main path, which in the daytime was usually busy with people and their pets. Toby stopped and stared along the muddy walkway. He couldn't see more than a few yards and they were cloaked in shadows, so that anyone could have easily hidden themselves.

"We should go back," said Sean, beside him.

"I'm just sure she knows something, whoever she is," said Toby.

"We aren't going to catch up with her now," reasoned Sean. "And I don't really want to be responsible for someone falling and breaking their neck if we did spot her and start racing after her again."

Toby suddenly felt stupid. "You're right," he said. "I don't know what came over me. It was the shock of thinking she was Miriam Darkwater. But why did she run?"

Sean took hold of his hand. "Come on," he said. "Let's get back."

Whether it was the affectionate touch of Sean's hand or the rush of adrenalin from seeing and giving chase to the red-haired woman, Toby wasn't sure, but he experienced a sudden wave of arousal. He pulled Sean toward him and planted a kiss on his lips.

"What was that for?" asked Sean.

"For coming with me," said Toby. "Most people would have left me to it."

"I did think about it," admitted Sean.

"But you didn't," said Toby, kissing him again, and this time Sean returned it. Soon their mouths were open and their tongues dancing.

Toby placed a hand on Sean's crotch, massaging his bulge until he was hard, growing hard himself as the kissing became increasingly passionate.

"You don't look so threatening now," came a voice from the shadows.

They jumped apart as the woman emerged from the trees at the edge of the pathway. She looked a little disheveled. Her cape was strewn with leaves and there was a twig caught in her red hair.

"Who are you?" she demanded. "And why the hell were you chasing me across Hampstead Heath at this time of night?"

"Why did you run away?" asked Toby.

"I saw the way you were staring at me and it made me nervous. Then I heard you running after me and I was scared. I thought you were a pair of muggers or worse. I wouldn't put it past Albert to hire a couple of goons to see me off. He knows people like that. Anyway, what would you do if two grown men started chasing after you?"

"I'm sorry," said Toby, taking a step toward her and holding out his hand. "I'm Toby and this is Sean. We both live at Darkwater House."

The woman looked at his hand, but didn't take it. Toby slipped it into his coat pocket as if he were embarrassed by it.

"You haven't answered my question," said the woman, who Toby now saw was only aged around fifty.

"It's hard to explain," said Toby. "I thought you were someone else...Alfred's mother."

"Really?" The woman raised her eyebrows. "You though I was my mother?"

"*Your* mother?" asked Toby.

"Yes. I'm Lilly Darkwater, Alfred's sister."

"Good to meet you," said Toby. He didn't risk holding out his hand again.

"And now I have another question," said Lilly. "Why the hell did you think I was my mother when she's been dead for ten years?"

Behind Toby, Sean coughed. "Could we maybe discuss this somewhere a bit warmer?" he said. "I'm freezing my bollocks off here."

Lilly seemed to relax a little at the sound of Sean's voice. His charm obviously worked on her too.

"I've a feeling your bollocks would have been even chillier if I hadn't spoken up when I did," said Lilly, one side of her mouth turning up in a smile.

"We could go back to the pub," suggested Sean, ignoring the remark and blushing.

"Would you join us for a drink?" asked Toby.

"I will if this young man lets me take his arm while we walk back across this bloody heath," said Lilly, approaching Sean and looping her arm through his.

"Not a problem," said Sean, although he looked taken aback.

"Don't worry," said Lilly, glancing at Toby. "I won't steal your boyfriend."

"We haven't actually had the boyfriend conversation yet," said Sean, leading the way back toward Darkwater House. "So, you never know your luck."

Lilly Darkwater laughed coquettishly.

Toby frowned and followed after them.

Chapter Fifteen

"I never got on with Alfred," said Lilly, taking a delicate sip from her small glass of white wine. "Or, more accurately, he never got on with me. He resented me from the day I was born. I took too much attention away from him. He was ten years old by the time I came along, and Daddy left only a year or so later, so I think he also blamed me for that. I think my mother did too. She certainly never showed me as much affection as she did Alfred, although the way he bleated on, you'd think I was her favorite."

Lilly was sitting across from Toby at a small table in the same pub they had left only thirty minutes earlier. Sean was sitting next to Toby, listening intently. Lilly had a commanding presence. Her vibrant hair framed a pale face sprinkled with freckles. On her, the paleness was attractive—not like Alfred's white skin, which had an unpleasant damp sheen to it, like cheese left in a hot room. In the heat of the pub, Lilly had removed her shawl to reveal a thin, tight-fitting pullover, which showed off a slim figure and surprisingly pert breasts.

Sean certainly seemed to approve, judging from the way he kept flicking his gaze down to her bust then back to her face.

"Things got so bad when I turned eleven years old that Mother sent me to boarding school in Scotland. It was an awful, bleak place—a great Victorian pile in the middle of nowhere and the other girls were mostly ghastly. Alfred was twenty-one by then, but he still behaved like a child. He never went to university or did anything normal men of his age were doing. He just hung around the house, waiting on Mother like hired help, lapping up any affection she threw his way. Anyway, you don't want to hear all that. You said on the way here that strange things were happening at the house. What sort of strange things?"

Toby glanced at Sean, who simply shrugged.

Lilly sighed. "Either tell me or let's drink up."

"I'm just not sure how to tell you," said Toby, "without you thinking I'm mad."

"Have you seen my mother?" asked Lilly.

"One of these days, someone is actually going to find that shocking," said Toby. "Yes, I have, a couple of times, and she seems very unhappy. No offense, but I'd say unhinged."

"She was a sandwich short of a picnic when she was alive," said Lilly. "At least, she turned that way after Daddy left. She tried to fill the void by renting out rooms at ridiculously low prices, but that just made Alfred even more unbearable, because he felt he was sharing her with the tenants too.

"Ironically, as he got older, it was Alfred who started to resent her. He blamed her for stopping him from having his own life and claimed she made it impossible for him to leave. But, if you ask me, he would never have had the guts. He certainly never had the guts to tell her he was gay, as if she'd have cared."

"Did you live at Darkwater House once you finished school?" asked Toby.

"God no!" replied Lilly. "I went to university in Bath, where I was very happy, and I met my future husband, Charles, there. We moved into a flat in Bath together after uni and stayed in the same city all our married life. He died a year ago, and I moved in with a dear friend who has a house in Camden Town. It's a bit hectic around there for me, but it's nice to have the company."

"So, you and Alfred never grew close, even once you were adults?" asked Sean.

"No. We grew even further apart. The final nail in the coffin was when I accused him of killing Mother."

There was a moment of heavy silence.

"Do you still think he did?" asked Toby.

"Don't you? Isn't that why we're here?"

Toby took a deep breath and told Lilly about his recent experience in the bath. She listened without interrupting.

"That sounds plausible," she said when he'd finished. "I can imagine Alfred murdering someone in that way. There would be no mess to clean up and a nice clean corpse. He was always prissy."

She was quiet for a while, taking a couple more mini sips of wine.

"I saw my mother too," she said eventually, looking down at the tabletop. "I've seen her a few times. The first time was just after she went missing. I insisted on staying at the house for a few days while the searches were going on. I was sitting at her dressing table when I saw her through the mirror, standing behind me. She looked miserable and she was shaking her head. Her hair was dripping wet.

"I put that time down to stress, but I saw her several times during that visit, and when I came to try to talk with Alfred last year, I saw her again from the road. She was standing at one of the first-floor windows staring out at me. Even from that distance, I could see her face was ravaged."

Toby shivered. "You were at the house a few days ago, weren't you?" he asked.

Lilly nodded. "I've been back several times over the past few months — firstly, to try and convince Albert to see me so that I can finally get a confession out of him, and secondly, to see Mother again. Albert refuses to open the door, but I have seen Mother looking out at me. I have to stand on the heath because you can't see the house well enough from the road."

"What makes you so sure he killed her?" asked Sean.

"His behavior in the last few years with Mother was very strange," said Lilly. "I'd visit every few months, much to his chagrin, and when he did speak to me, it was to accuse me of leaving him to care for Mother, of how his life had been ruined because of my selfishness. He made no mention of the fact that I'd had to leave home because of his pure hatred toward me.

"Even when he was in his late teens and early twenties, he would throw tantrums if I appeared to be getting more attention than he was. It was like he was possessed sometimes. And here he was blaming me and Mother for all his woes. He started saying that he despised her, that she was a leech, sucking the life out of him. That's when I started to get concerned.

"But what could I do? Mother was physically fine and still independent in terms of being able to look after herself. Mentally she was fragile, but that was the norm.

"When he called me to say she was missing, I knew he was hiding something. He didn't want me to come, but I wouldn't take no for an answer. He didn't have the security gate back then, so getting into the house was easier. I just turned up at his front door with my suitcase and pushed my way in.

"I got quite friendly with one of the tenants, a woman called Sheila. We kept in touch for a few years and she told me that Alfred had started renting to a certain type of person."

"What do you mean?" asked Toby.

"Don't take this the wrong way," said Lilly, "but Sheila said she thought Alfred wanted rid of her because she wasn't miserable enough."

"What?" asked Toby and Sean together.

"According to Sheila, Alfred was gradually replacing the existing tenants with new ones, and all the new tenants were deeply unhappy. Sheila said she thought Alfred wanted to surround himself with unhappy people, that he somehow fed off their misery. I didn't want to offend Sheila, but the truth was, most people who came to live at Darkwater House were unhappy, even during Mother's time, Sheila included. But I don't think Mother deliberately surrounded herself with misery. I think she genuinely wanted to help. No doubt, Albert would tell a different story."

Toby and Sean looked at each other.

"Did she say if he deliberately did things to ensure people stayed unhappy?" asked Toby.

Lilly nodded. "She had her suspicions. She even thought he'd let himself into her flat when she wasn't there and rearranged the furniture to unsettle her. She moved out eventually and we lost touch."

"I think he's still creeping into people's flats," said Toby. "I think he may have stolen Susan's mobile phone from her flat, which explains why her son couldn't get through to her."

"Why do you think that?" asked Sean.

"When I was at Alfred's flat, I heard a mobile phone ringing, even though Alfred claims not to have one. I think it may have been Susan's," said Toby. "Susan was a tenant who recently committed suicide," he added for Lilly's benefit.

"How sad," said Lilly. "And you think my brother deliberately stole her mobile phone so that her son couldn't get in touch?"

"I got the impression that the relationship with her son was a bit strained, but he came to visit her the day she killed herself. She didn't answer her intercom, and he couldn't get through to her by phone. I think Alfred deliberately disconnected her intercom so that she would think her son hadn't come, and that she then got blind drunk and decided life wasn't worth living."

"Poor woman," said Lilly. "And if you're right, I'm even more convinced that Alfred was capable of killing our mother."

"He's tried to spoil things between us too," said Toby. "I won't go into detail, but he definitely doesn't like the fact that Sean and I are getting on."

"He doesn't want you to be happy," said Lilly. "Your misery is what makes him content."

"Did the police never investigate your mother's death?" asked Sean, leaning across the table. "Surely your brother must have been a suspect."

"They asked him questions and they must have searched the house, but he was never arrested or charged, so they obviously didn't find any evidence. I guess elderly women go missing quite often. I should have done more back then, but my husband fell ill at the same time and I had to get back to Bath and be there for him. Caring for Charles took over my life for years, and I tried to convince myself that I'd been wrong about Alfred, but in the last year since Charles died, I've had time to think about it again. I'm sure my brother is a murderer."

"So, what do we do now?" asked Toby.

"We need proof," said Lilly. "Then we can bring the police in."

"By proof you mean…" began Toby.

"A body," said Lilly. "Or bones by now, I suppose."

"Where would you suggest looking?" asked Sean.

"I'd start with the cellar," said Lilly. "I don't think the police even knew there was a cellar. The lift used to go down to that level when it was all one house, but once Mother started renting out rooms, she had that button for the cellar disconnected. Giving tenants access to a basement full of wine isn't the best idea. There's a small door in the kitchen that leads down there. Mother used to keep a spare key on the bottom stair."

"I'm sure I could reconnect the lift button," said Sean. "I did some training as an electrician before I decided on carpentry."

"Handy *and* handsome," said Lilly.

"Isn't he?" agreed Toby.

"Here's my number," said Lilly, plucking a card from somewhere and sliding it across the table. "Keep me updated."

"We will," said Toby, snatching up the card before Sean could.

Chapter Sixteen

When Toby woke in Sean's bed the next morning, he thought first of the strange events of the previous evening, then of how he and Sean had made love when they'd gotten home. They had sat in the living room at first, talking over what Lilly had told them, but soon they had started kissing and undressing each other, almost tripping over themselves in the rush to get to the bedroom. Sean had fucked Toby again, first doggy style, his cock penetrating deeper than ever, then face-to-face, taking it slow. Even when they had both reached orgasm the second time, they had continued to kiss for at least half an hour, remaining hard but too tired to make love again.

Sean's side of the bed was empty and Toby momentarily panicked, but then his lover entered the room, holding out a steaming mug of coffee, dressed in faded jeans, a tight white T-shirt and a brown leather tool belt. On his feet he wore scuffed work boots.

"Please tell me you have time to fuck me while dressed like that," said Toby, reaching out and stroking Sean's bulge.

"Afraid not," said Sean, placing the coffee on the bedside table and bending down for a kiss. "My mate is picking me up outside in five minutes, so I have to run. Stay in bed as long as you want. It's still early. And don't do anything about what we discussed last night until we've had time to talk again and plan things properly. I don't want to come home and find you've electrocuted yourself in the lift — or worse, been taken hostage by Albert and forced to be his sex slave."

Toby scowled. "Yes, death by electrocution would definitely be preferable to that."

"I'll see you later," said Sean.

"Good luck!" called Toby as his lover walked away, already planning a sex session with Sean wearing the boots and tool belt.

Toby drank his coffee then climbed from the bed, walking through to the kitchen still naked. He put the kettle on. He'd have another coffee here before heading back to his place. There was something nice about being naked in Sean's flat. As the kettle began to boil, Toby heard a key in the front door.

"Sean?" He walked out to the hallway.

"Oh, hello, Toby." Albert Darkwater gave Toby's naked body a long, lingering appraisal. "What a shame you cut things short the other evening. It would have been quite a show."

Toby refused to be embarrassed. It was Albert who had let himself in uninvited. Why should he be made to feel awkward?

"What are you doing here?" he asked, making no attempt to cover himself.

"I could ask you the same," said Albert, taking a step closer. Toby stood his ground, hands on hips.

"I'm here because I spent last night with Sean," said Toby. "He knows I'm in his flat, but does he know you are?"

"I'm the landlord," said Albert. "I have every right to let myself in."

"Not without prior warning you don't," said Toby, hoping that was right.

"I'm just making a routine check to make sure the flat is being properly cared for," said Albert.

Toby shrugged. "Go ahead," he said, returning to the kitchen to finish making coffee. He could feel Albert staring at his arse as he walked away, but he wasn't going to show his discomfort.

"If you're making coffee, I'll have one," said Albert, following Toby into the kitchen.

"I didn't offer you one," said Toby, pouring boiling water into the cafetière.

"Well, if it's too much trouble," said Albert, blatantly staring at Toby's cock.

"Not at all," replied Toby with a grimace. "Milk and sugar?"

"Yes to milk, no to sugar," replied Albert. "I'm sweet enough."

"Of course you are," said Toby.

"You know, you could finish giving me that show now," said Albert. "You're halfway there."

"There won't be any shows, Albert," said Toby, placing the cafetière and two mugs on the breakfast bar where Albert sat. Toby straddled the stool next to him, his cock and balls hanging over the edge of the seat. He was starting to enjoy the sport of letting Albert see what he couldn't ever touch.

Remember, he may be a killer, he told himself.

But Toby was also thinking that while Albert was drooling over his body, he was a captive audience or, more accurately, a captive talker who might reveal more than intended while his mind was elsewhere.

"I saw something online yesterday about your poor mother," Toby said as he pushed down on the cafetière plunger. "I hadn't realized she'd gone missing. That must have been such a stressful time."

Albert fidgeted on his stool. Toby tried to ignore the obvious tenting in his gray trousers as he poured coffee into his mug.

"Yes, it was," said Albert. "Why were you looking up information about my mother on the Internet?"

"I was just curious about the history of the house, and I stumbled across a couple of old news stories from the local paper," said Toby, standing and bending down to open the fridge door. "I forgot the milk," he said, giving Albert plenty of time to admire his spread arse cheeks before standing upright.

"Say when," he said, pouring milk into Albert's mug, aware of how close to the old man's leg his cock was dangling but not allowing himself to flinch. This time he was in control. Albert made no attempt to touch him.

"When!" blurted Albert, just before the mug overflowed.

Toby sat back down and poured his own coffee. "You must remember seeing her off to the pond that morning like it was yesterday."

"I do," said Albert. "I warned her not to go. I said it was too cold, but she never took any notice of me."

"So, do you think she drowned?" asked Toby, swiveling around on his stool to face Albert, his legs parted as far as possible.

Please God, don't let him try to touch me.

Albert blushed and looked like he might fall off his own stool. His hand was shaking as he lifted his mug to his lips.

"I can't think of any other explanation," said Albert. "I believe she jumped into the water and the cold made her heart stop. I don't understand why they couldn't find her body. It would have been good to have had that closure."

"Did you have to wait seven years for her to be declared officially dead?" asked Toby.

Albert shook his head. "That law changed in 2013, so after four years, I applied to the High Court for a declaration of death or some legal document. That was when it became official, although I knew she was dead long before that."

"Why were you so sure?" asked Toby.

"I'm her son. I could sense it. Plus, why else would a seventy-something-year-old woman not come home? She was hardly likely to have run away with a secret lover, was she?"

"I didn't know her," said Toby. "I don't know what kind of woman she was."

"What do you mean by that?" demanded Albert, slopping coffee onto his full lap.

"Nothing at all," Toby assured him.

"She was a good person," said Albert, placing his mug on the breakfast bar. "I looked after her for years when she lost the plot over my father leaving us."

"I'm sure you did, and it must have been hard. You must have had to put a lot of your own life on hold."

"I certainly did."

"No one would blame you for being a bit resentful of that," said Toby.

"Who said I was resentful?" demanded Albert. "I didn't say that. You did."

Toby raised a hand, palm toward Albert. "Calm down, Albert. I wasn't suggesting anything. Her death was hardly your fault."

"What?" Albert stood, his face quivering with rage now. "Why would you say that? And why are you sitting in front of me naked?"

"I thought you wanted to see me naked, Albert," said Toby, also standing. "I would have put some clothes on if I'd known you were so easily offended."

"You're a cocktease," snapped Albert. "That's what you are! Flashing your wares in front of me then pretending you don't want me touching them."

Albert was backing toward the front door. "I'll deal with you," he said, growing redder. "I'll bloody deal with you, you cock-teasing prick!"

"What will you do?" asked Toby. "Drown me in the bath?"

Albert froze for a second, glaring at Toby with mix of shock, fear and loathing.

"Shut up!" he yelled. "Just shut up, you cocktease!"

And he turned and ran to the door, flinging it open and slamming it closed behind him.

Chapter Seventeen

Much as he hated to admit it, knowing how much Albert desired him gave Toby a perverse pleasure. He felt as though he had redressed the balance of power between them after it had tipped so far in Albert's favor the night Toby had visited his flat. Toby wasn't sure, though, how Sean would feel about his deliberately parading naked in front of Albert in order to unsettle him into revealing more than he intended. As interrogation techniques went, it was unusual.

He was also concerned that he might have pushed Albert too far. He had seemed unhinged when he'd left Sean's flat. Whatever he and Sean planned to do in order to uncover any secrets Darkwater House was hiding, Toby thought they needed to act quickly. He had visions of Albert sneaking into his bedroom at night and slitting his throat while he slept, hissing "cocktease!" as the blade sliced through his jugular.

Toby spent the rest of the day working on features, although it was difficult to focus. Sometimes he would think someone was watching him. On several occasions he turned, expecting to see the ghost of Albert's mother staring at him from the other side of the room. But there was never anyone there.

At six o'clock he heard Sean arriving home — the tread of his heavy work boots on the hall carpet and the sound of his key in the door. Toby didn't rush straight over. Sean would be tired after a day working. He'd want to strip out of his grimy clothes and shower.

After being patient for ten minutes, Toby sent Sean a text. They'd finally swapped numbers the night before.

I think Albert is losing the plot. When do you think we should check out the cellar?

Toby waited.
Five minutes later a text came back.

Sorry… Was in the shower. I saw Albert in the hall earlier. He was going to see a friend in Edgware, so guessing we have time this evening. Want to meet me by the lift in five minutes?

Toby was at the lift within three. He had already called it and was keeping the door open with his foot. When Sean emerged from his flat, he was wearing a loose gray jumper, a pair of gray jogging bottoms and trainers. His hair was still wet from the shower.

"You're keen," he said, producing a screwdriver from up the sleeve of his pullover. "I checked the panel on the way up. I think this is the right size. You just keep the door open so we don't have to explain what we're doing to anyone else."

"Yes, sir," said Toby, as Sean crouched down by the button panel and began to loosen the screws that held it in place.

"Let's just hope he only disconnected the wiring and didn't totally remove it," he said.

"You're in a very serious mood," said Toby.

"We're hot-wiring a lift so that we can trespass in someone's cellar, looking for their dead mother," said Sean, without looking up.

"Fair enough," replied Toby.

"We're in luck," mumbled Sean. Two minutes later he was replacing the panel and standing.

"Shall we?" he said, pointing to the now-illuminated 'B for basement' button.

Toby pressed it before he had the chance to change his mind. The door closed and the lift shuddered into motion.

No one else tried to join them on the way down, but there was a good chance someone might call the lift once they had alighted in the cellar. But as long as it wasn't Albert, it didn't really matter. Toby couldn't imagine any of the tenants had a good relationship with the creep. Why would they bother mentioning to him that the basement button had been working for the first time since they'd moved in? They might not even notice.

"We're here," said Sean, his tone ominous, and the lift door opened into almost total darkness. Only the first few feet of the cellar were lit by the soft glow from inside the lift.

"Shit," said Toby. "I didn't bring a torch."

Sean shook his head, tutted and produced a small torch from his other sleeve. For its size, it produced a powerful glow. Sean was already outside the lift, shining the beam on the wall next to the door.

"What are you doing?" asked Toby, joining him and already wishing he had worn a coat or jumper. The cellar was cold.

"I'm checking to see if there is a working button down here to call the lift if we need to. Otherwise, we'll need to jam the door with something."

As if it had heard Sean, the lift pinged and the door began to slide closed.

"Quick!" snapped Sean, and Toby once again blocked the door from closing with his foot.

"Well?" he asked. "Is there a button?"

"Yes," said Sean.

"Good." Toby removed his foot.

"But it's totally rusted and not working," said Sean, as the lift juddered upward.

"What?" Toby glared at Sean. "Are you serious?"

Sean glared back. "Yes, I'm serious. Why did you let it go?"

"Let's search the cellar then worry about how we're going to get out," said Toby, sounding calmer than he felt.

"Great plan," said Sean, now shining the torch beam across the cavernous space.

"Did you have a bad day at work?" asked Toby, walking tentatively forward.

"No," said Sean. "I'm just tired. I get grumpy when I'm tired. Plus, we're trapped in a cellar which no one but Albert even knows exists, so we're probably going to die down here."

"Perhaps we should limit our friendship to weekend dates," said Toby.

Sean hushed him, which Toby would normally have objected to, but these were unusual circumstances.

So far, all Toby could see were piles of boxes or crates, all covered in a sheen of dust. He could hear a constant dripping sound, and the concrete floor was dotted with puddles. There was also a prevailing smell of damp.

Finally they found a set of light switches and bare bulbs flickered into life across the vast space.

"Jesus," gasped Sean, switching off his torch. "This place is huge. And it has wine like a real cellar."

Against the far wall, Toby saw shelves filled with his favorite beverage. He wandered over, scanning the dust-coated bottes. Although he consumed huge amounts of it, he was no wine expert. He'd learned it was worth spending eight pounds on a bottle rather than five if he wanted something that would go down fairly smoothly, and that he preferred merlot to other varieties, but that was pretty much the extent of his knowledge.

He walked on past the wine racks to an area that contained a large desk — a hulking great thing from the Victorian age, totally out of keeping with the rest of the furniture in Albert's flat. No wonder it had been abandoned down here in this dank place. On top of it stood an equally ugly object — a lamp with a base made out of shells. It was like something Toby's mother would have bought from one of the tacky gift shops in Spain.

"I'm guessing this was an unwanted Christmas present," Toby said, nodding at the monstrosity.

"Hurry up!" snapped Sean.

Toby began opening the desk drawers. They were filled with paperwork—old bills, solicitor's letters and what looked like the deeds to a property.

"Shine the torch over here," directed Toby. "The light is crap in this corner."

Sean stood close behind him, peering at the document over his shoulder. He clicked on the torch and shone it onto the deeds as Toby spread them out across the desktop. Sure enough, they were the deeds to a sprawling property, but it wasn't Darkwater House. Printed at the top of the document was the name Heath View Mansion, and the date 1853.

"Where is this?" asked Toby.

"Here, maybe," said Sean. "Or here before they built this place. Albert mentioned there'd been a dilapidated house here when his parents bought the plot. These must be the deeds to that property."

Toby folded the deeds up and slipped them down the front of his jeans.

"What are you doing?" asked Sean.

"They may be useful," said Toby. "Who knows what they could reveal about the grounds?"

"Clever," said Sean, giving Toby's arse a pat—something Toby would normally find condescending, but from Sean it felt comforting.

Sean made to move on, but Toby spotted something else in the drawer...a book.

"Wait! Shine the torch over here again," he whispered.

The beam fell on the inside of the drawer and Toby saw that the book was, in fact, a diary—the year inscribed on the front cover in gold was 1982. He grabbed it and opened it to the first page. Written in swirling handwriting was the name 'Albert Darkwater'.

"This I have to read," said Toby, tucking the diary under his arm and sliding the drawer closed.

They continued to search the cellar, scanning walls for any sign of newer plasterwork, evidence that bricks had been removed and replaced, a body concealed behind them. Perhaps they had both just watched too many crime movies. An hour later, they arrived back at the lift, having discovered nothing suspicious.

"Looks like Lilly was wrong," said Toby. "And now we have to worry about how the fuck we get out of here."

"We should turn the lights out," said Sean, walking over to the panel of switches. For a moment the cellar was doused in total darkness. Then Sean's face was illuminated by the torch beam.

"Hurry," said Toby, suddenly uneasy standing in the darkness in this dripping, vast cold space.

A familiar juddering sound made them both jump.

"It's the lift," said Toby, turning to face the closed door. The panel of lights above it which would have shown which floor the elevator was on wasn't working, but the sudden ping announced the lift's arrival.

"Shit!" hissed Toby, leaping to one side and ducking behind a tower of crates. The torch beam disappeared with an almost inaudible click and the lift door slid open.

Through a gap between two crates, Toby could see Albert framed in the lift entrance. His hands were planted on his jutting hips and he was muttering to himself. He stepped out of the lift and reached into a dark alcove just beside it. With a series of clicks the lights flickered on across the cellar. There was obviously more than one set of switches. Toby peered toward where Sean had been standing just a few seconds earlier, but he had obviously managed to hide.

Why is Albert even here? He couldn't have got to Edgware and back that quickly. His plans had obviously changed. Or, thought Toby with a sinking feeling, had he just fed Sean a lie about going to visit his friend, knowing they had something planned?

"Is someone there?" called Albert, his voice bouncing off the walls. He sounded unsure, nervous. "Hello!" he called again.

Toby tried to control his breathing. To him it sounded loud enough to wake the dead, as did the beating of his heart. But Albert headed away from where he was crouched, glancing around him as he went. Soon he disappeared from view, but Toby could hear his footsteps echoing throughout the cellar as he went.

Suddenly the lights went out and a second later someone was pulling Toby from his hiding place. For a hideous moment, he thought it was Albert, but then he heard Albert calling from some way off. "Who's there?" and the sound of crates toppling where the old man must have collided with them in the dark.

"Come on!" hissed Sean, dragging Toby into the lift and slamming his palm against the button for the ground floor. It seemed to take an age for the door to close. They huddled against the panel of buttons, trying to keep their faces out of sight should Albert emerge from the dense blackness of the cellar. They heard a scrambling sound and pained grunting.

"Maybe he's hurt," whispered Toby, as the lift door slid closed.

"Tough shit," said Sean, who was crouching down, unscrewing the button panel. It only took a second to detach the wiring and he began to reaffix the metal cover. The lift door slid open. Gita the nurse was standing with her back to them, rummaging in her handbag, then looking across the hall toward the front door as if she thought she might have dropped something. Toby shifted so that he stood in front of Sean as he finished screwing the panel back into place.

Gita turned and let out a startled yelp.

"Hi," said Sean, now standing, screwdriver concealed up his sleeve. "You okay?"

"Yes," said the nurse. "I just can't find my keys. I think I may have left them in my front door."

"Hope you find them," said Toby, stepping out of the lift and pulling Sean with him.

"Thanks," said Gita, distractedly, prodding the button for her floor.

"Where are we going?" asked Sean.

"Well, there wasn't room for all three of us in the lift, and she would have thought we had just come down from our floor, wouldn't she? So why would we have been going back up again?"

"True," said Sean, walking toward the stairs. "Well, I don't know about you, but I need a drink."

"I always need a drink," said Toby, although for the first time in a while, he didn't actually care if he had one or not.

Chapter Eighteen

They spread the deeds they had found in the cellar across the island in Sean's kitchen. Sean was swigging from a bottle of beer, while Toby had opted for a coffee, as he wanted to keep a clear head.

"Do you think he knows it was us?" he asked.

Sean shrugged. "If he confronts us, we just say the lift took us to the cellar and we were curious. It's quite possible the wires could have reconnected accidently. He doesn't know we suspect anything, does he?"

Toby recalled his argument with Albert that morning.

'What will you do, drown me in the bath?'

"He may have an inkling," he said. "I could maybe pop down later, just to see how he reacts, and also check that he survived the fall in the cellar. He is in his sixties."

"We think the guy might have murdered his mother, remember?" said Sean. "Let's not start getting all touchy feely about him."

"Plus, he probably helped drive Susan to suicide," added Toby.

Sean tapped a spot on the deeds. "What's this?" he said, squinting in an effort to read the tiny print. Toby pushed him to one side and peered at the area he was indicating.

"It says it's a well," Toby said. "I've never noticed a well in the back garden. Mind you, I've hardly spent any time out there. Why bother with a garden when you have the entire heath at your disposal?"

"It would be a good place to dispose of a body," said Sean.

Toby nodded. "We just need to wait for Albert to head out again then go explore."

"You make this sound like an adventure," said Sean, and he sounded critical.

"Well, it is," said Toby. "I feel like a detective and you're my trusty sidekick."

Sean laughed. "Yeah right, I'm the sidekick. I don't think so."

"Maybe you should get some sleep," suggested Toby, folding up the deeds. "We can't do much more tonight. Albert will be on his guard now that he knows someone was snooping in the cellar."

"I am knackered," said Sean. "And I have a full-on day tomorrow too."

"Get to bed," said Toby, kissing Sean on his bristled cheek. He loved the rough texture of it against his lips. "I'll speak to you tomorrow."

"Don't do anything stupid while I'm at work," called Sean, as Toby left.

"I can't promise that," whispered Toby.

As he pushed his front door key into the lock, Toby sensed someone watching him from the end of the passage near the lift. He turned, prepared to see the phantom, but it was Albert who stood glaring at him. He looked almost as terrifying as his dead mother. His thin hair was caked in grime, his face streaked with it. His mouth was quivering as he fought through the rage to speak.

"It was you, wasn't it," he finally shrieked. "You and your queer friend."

"What?" Toby turned to face his landlord, not wanting to seem afraid.

"You were in the cellar, snooping around."

"What cellar? I didn't know we had a cellar."

"Don't play dumb." Albert took a few steps toward Toby but stopped, his whole body tremoring with anger. "What if I hadn't had a key to the door into my kitchen? I'd have been trapped down there. Is that what you wanted?"

"I really have no idea what you're talking about," said Toby. "But you're obviously shaken up. Did you want to come in and sit down for a bit?"

Toby was holding Albert's diary behind his back, ready to slip it down the back of his jeans should Albert get any closer. He was glad he'd left the deeds at Sean's place. Concealing that unwieldy document and the diary would have been impossible.

"Fuck you!" spat Albert. "Stay away from my cellar and my flat."

As he turned to march away, Albert stumbled, reaching out to steady himself against a wall. He paused before continuing at a slower pace. He looked old and vulnerable. Toby felt a pang of guilt. What if he'd gotten it wrong and Albert was innocent?

He tried to blackmail you into stripping for him, Toby reminded himself, and he felt better about things.

By the time he climbed into bed, Toby was exhausted, but he wanted to read some of Albert's diary before he went to sleep. He plumped up his pillows to form a comfortable backrest and took the fake-leather-bound volume from the bedside table, opening it to the first entry.

January 1, 1982

So, it's a new year, but what does that really mean to me? I thought I'd start keeping a diary, as I need somewhere to give vent to what I'm really feeling. I have to keep up a front for Mother. I don't want her knowing how unhappy I am.

The worst thing about the Christmas holidays is that she has been here. Two weeks of her irritating cheeriness, although at least it sounds as though she hates boarding school. I think she is being bullied, which makes me happy. At least she will be going back to Scotland in a couple of days. I watched her sleeping the other night and it was all I could do not to smother her fat little face with a pillow.

"Jesus," whispered Toby. "He really did hate Lilly."

He scanned the next few entries, which were all of a similar nature — the morose, meandering thoughts of a depressed twenty-something-year-old with no life. Then on the entry for the twenty-third of April, a sentence caught his attention.

I had sex for the first time today.

Toby sat up straighter, shifting into a more comfortable position, and continued reading.

I thought it would never happen, but I finally had sex with another man. I can never let anyone else read this. I will need to find a really good place to hide it. I can just imagine what

156

Lilly would do with this kind of information. But I need to record it, because I never want to forget a second of how it felt.

His name is John Gowerford, and he's a bit of a gangster – well, more than a bit of a gangster... I think he's fully-fledged!

I was in the West End clothes shopping. Mother said my current wardrobe was looking dated and gave me some money to buy some new attire. After I'd bought some trousers and a couple of shirts on Oxford Street, I decided to have a wander around Soho. On one of the side streets, I noticed a pink triangle in the corner of the front window of an old-fashioned-looking pub. I've never been into a gay pub before. I've always been too scared. But today I decided to be brave. I'm twenty-three, for God's sake. I need a sex life.

I hesitated at the door to the pub for a moment, then pushed it open and walked into a smog of cigarette smoke. There was loud music playing, I think it was something by that band Culture Club, although all modern music sounds the same to me. I focused on the bar and kept walking without looking around me, although I could tell there were quite a few people standing about and some sitting at tables near the window.

The barman was friendly, which set me at ease, and I ordered a gin and tonic. I was too nervous to try to find a seat, so I just stayed at the bar, still not really looking around. I was about to down my drink and leave when he sidled up next to me.

He was wearing a suit, which struck me as unusual in such an informal atmosphere. I could see in the mirror behind the bar that he was handsome and a lot older than me. It turns out he's in his forties. He ordered a pint of lager and, while he waited, he caught my eye in the mirror and winked. I blushed and looked away. Luckily, he was not deterred and next thing I knew, a fresh gin and tonic was slid in front of me and he was introducing himself. He is so handsome that I found it hard to look him straight in the face. He has dark hair with streaks of gray running through the sides. His eyes are gray and bore right into you. He's not tall, probably about five feet nine, but he has broad shoulders and a slim waist. I took all this in very quickly as he suggested we sit at a table in a dark corner at the back of the pub.

Toby tried to imagine the young Albert as he read. He couldn't help but feel for the attractive twenty-three-year-old meeting his first lover and experiencing all the excitement that came with that. The page of the diary for that date was already full, but Albert had inserted several extra lined pieces of paper so that he could continue the story of that eventful day. Toby read how the pair had chatted for around an hour in the pub, until, finally, John had placed a hand on Albert's knee and suggested they head to his flat, which he said was just a short walk away. Toby imagined young Albert nervously joining his older man on the walk through Soho. The flat was above a sleazy sex shop, accessed via a narrow, winding stairway, but when John had opened the front door, Albert had been pleasantly surprised by the property itself. John obviously had some wealth, judging by the way the apartment was furnished and decorated.

He offered me a drink, and I said yes, but he didn't even bother going to prepare it. Instead he pulled me to him and kissed me. I just opened my mouth and let his tongue do all the work. I've never kissed a man until him. The only times I've kissed before have been with girls who I had no interest in and I'd just waggled my tongue around, hoping they wouldn't notice my heart wasn't in it. But I didn't want to do this with John. He asked me what was wrong and I admitted I was nervous. He told me to relax and kissed me again. This time I responded, and it all came naturally. He began to undress me, pulling my jumper over my head and unbuttoning my shirt, until I was topless. He kissed my nipples and I felt a charge run from them right through me. I tried to unbutton his shirt too, but my hands were shaking too much and he had to do it himself. He shrugged off his jacket and shirt, revealing a broad, hairy chest, which I rubbed my face again, breathing in his manly scent. My cock has never been so hard.

Toby was growing hard himself. If he hadn't seen the photograph of Albert when he was young, he might not have found the account such a turn-on, but imagining that handsome young man from the picture getting more and more aroused as his older lover undressed him was proving to be an erotic experience. Toby tried to push all thoughts of Albert as he was now from his mind as he read on. Eventually he came to the part where young Albert had his first experience being fucked.

At first it hurt, even though he'd smeared my hole with plenty of lube. It was as if my arse was rejecting that thick cock of his, my muscles pushing against it. He withdrew and told me it was fine, just to relax. Finally it slid into me and I was filled with warmth and begging him to fuck me as hard as he could...and he did. I came quicker than I meant to, shooting all over his stomach. He pulled his cock out of me and masturbated until he came too, covering me in thick globs of cum. It felt so good. I smeared myself with it then licked my fingers as I stared into those gray eyes.

Toby's hand strayed to his own stiff cock.
No, he may be young and cute here, but it's still Albert!
He pulled his hand from under the quilt and continued flicking through the diary pages.

Several months into the year, another entry caught Toby's eye.

August 3, 1982

John is married. I'm broken-hearted. I genuinely thought he loved me. All those nights spent in his flat in Soho making love and he had a wife waiting at home – his real home.

He told me he doesn't love her, that she is just for appearances, that someone in his line of work can't be openly gay. He says he cares about me more than he has ever cared about her, but I don't trust him anymore. How can I?

I left in tears and I've been crying ever since. Mother knows something is wrong, but I keep telling her I'm fine. Maybe if I didn't have to stay here making sure she doesn't do something stupid, I might be able to meet someone decent, settle down with a normal guy who isn't a gangster and married.

The fact is, even if John wasn't married and was looking for a more serious relationship, I could never leave Mother on her own, not the way she is. Without me here, she'd kill herself within a few weeks.

The bitterness which Toby believed had led to Albert killing his mother was already evident, even as far back as 1982. Toby wondered what had happened to the blossoming, but seemingly doomed, relationship with John. He flicked through the remainder of the diary. Most of it was filled with angst-ridden entries about how much he missed John. Then Toby noticed a change of mood.

November 8, 1982

I met up with John today for the first time since he'd told me about his wife. The good news is, she is ill – really ill – and has gone to live in a special home where she can be cared for. He didn't explain exactly what was wrong with her, but it's something that means she can't move on her own, and he says he doesn't have time to look after her.

He says I can come and visit him at his main home now if I want. It's a big house out in the suburbs somewhere. I still have to be discreet, because some of the neighbors are friends with his wife and will be visiting her in the home, but he says he wants to make love to me in their marital bed, to show me that it's me he loves, not her. I've agreed to go. I'm going to call him at the flat tomorrow to get the address.

I know I will end up getting hurt, but I love him, so what else can I do?

Toby turned the page, genuinely intrigued to know how things would develop, but the rest of the diary was empty. Maybe young Albert's life had become too busy for him to find time to record it on those pages.

Chapter Nineteen

Toby had expected to lie awake for hours, his mind racing with recent events and the content of the diary, but he fell into a deep sleep. When he woke, it was daylight. He sat up, feeling instantly awake and refreshed. He glanced at the clock next to the bed and was shocked to see it was already eight-thirty. He couldn't remember when he'd last slept so well.

While he drank his first coffee, he stared out of the living -room window at the back garden. He'd not paid it much attention until now. With the heath as a backdrop, the garden faded into obscurity in comparison. It wasn't huge, no more than fifty feet long and not much wider than the house itself, but it was extremely overgrown, with a mature weeping willow overshadowing much of it, the ground a tangle of brambles and weeds. Any well would have been long concealed. If they were going to search in that wasteland, they'd need gardening gloves and something to hack through the undergrowth.

Toby showered and dressed then headed out to find the nearest garden center. In the communal hallway, he bumped into Albert, who was also heading out. The old man glowered at him.

"Morning!" chirped Toby. "Are you feeling better today?"

"No!" snapped Albert. "And don't go trying to break into my flat while I'm out. I've set the alarm, so you'll be talking to the police if you do."

Toby couldn't recall seeing an alarm system in Albert's flat.

"I've no intention of breaking into your home," he said, still with forced brightness.

Toby waited for Albert to disappear through the gate at the end of the drive before leaving the house. As he closed the front door, he hesitated. This would be the perfect time to investigate the garden, with Albert away and plenty of daylight left. If he wasted time buying gloves and tools, Albert would be home again. He waited a few seconds to ensure that Albert wasn't going to come back, then walked briskly around the side of the house. There was a tall wooden gate blocking access to the back garden and it was locked, but one good shove with his shoulder and the gate swung open. Toby kicked the dislodged bolt into the overgrown verge that ran along the perimeter fence and pushed the gate closed behind him.

The garden was even more jungle-like than he'd thought. The brambles and weeds grew to waist height and there was a thick layer of mulch on the ground. He could hear creatures scurrying through the undergrowth, probably running from him. He pictured the deeds and where the well had been situated in the plans. It was hard to pinpoint its exact location, because the deeds featured the original property, not Darkwater House, which meant that the garden may have been bigger when they were drawn up. He knew the well had been set toward the rear of the garden, so at least there was no danger that Darkwater House had been built over it.

Toby trampled over the snagging brambles, making slow progress, until he reached the spot where he thought the well should be. There was no sign of it. He wasn't even sure what he should be looking for. Would it be a raised structure like a fairy-tale wishing well, or flat against the ground with a wooden cover to stop people from falling into it? If the latter, then finding it would be a major challenge. He began walking with deliberately heavy footsteps, hoping to detect a hollow sound that would betray the existence of the well. Nothing.

He was about to give up when he spotted something beneath a particularly dense bramble patch. It looked like a metal hoop. He crouched down to get a closer look, reaching into the brambles and touching the object. It was indeed metal, and when he tugged at it with the tips of his fingers, it remained firm, suggesting that it was attached to something—a wooden cover perhaps. Toby withdrew his hand, wincing as thorns scratched at his skin. At least now he knew where the well was, but he'd have to come back with something to cut through those brambles and some gloves to stop his hands from being shredded.

He made his way back to the side gate, peering out to make sure his exit wouldn't be witnessed by anyone. He pulled the gate closed behind him, wedging a stone under it so that it wouldn't swing open too easily. As he jogged up the driveway, he wondered if he had time to buy what he needed and get back to the garden before Albert returned.

It was worth a try.

* * * *

By the time he got back to Darkwater House, carrying a bag containing two pairs of ultra-thick gardening gloves, two sets of secateurs and a sturdy torch, Toby was beginning to have second thoughts about tackling the task of uncovering the well alone. He recalled Sean's warning not to do anything stupid while he was at work, and there was a good reason why he'd bought two sets of gloves and cutters. But if he waited for Sean to be free, it could be days before they had a chance to investigate the well.

The first thing he needed to do was see if Albert was back. If he was, that was the decision made. He pressed the bell for Albert's flat next to the outside gate and waited. After a few seconds he pressed it again. There was still no answer.

"Let's do this," Toby said aloud as he punched in the security code.

He half-walked, half-ran down the driveway to the side gate. Adrenaline spurred him on as he trampled over the brambles to the spot where he had seen the metal hoop. He slipped on a pair of gloves and began to snip and tug his way through the barricade of thorny stems.

It took half an hour to clear the vegetation from the area around the loop, then he needed to scoop up the two-inch-thick layer of sodden leaves. But it was worth the effort, because there, as he'd hoped, was the circular wooden cover. He took a deep breath and pulled at the metal ring. The cover didn't budge. Sighing, Toby cut back more of the brambles that may have been hampering his efforts then tried again, gripping the handle with both hands and yanking with all his strength. Without warning, the cover came free and Toby toppled backward. The piece of wood fell onto the ground a few feet away, revealing a circular opening. Toby crawled over to the well and peered down. It was too dark to see anything. He took a deep breath, but there was no smell of decaying flesh, just the tang of dank water, rotten vegetation and maybe a hint of sewage. He retrieved the torch, which he'd had the foresight to buy batteries for, from the bag and shone it into the opening. He could see no obvious obstructions, nothing that resembled a pile of bones or a mummy-like corpse, preserved in the damp atmosphere. And looking at the width of the well, Toby wasn't even convinced a body would fit down there.

Resigned, Toby puled the piece of wood back into place and did his best to cover it with the severed pieces of vegetation he had piled around it. He couldn't imagine Albert spent much time out here, not judging by the state of the garden, so he hoped his snooping would go unnoticed.

Something stirred in the undergrowth a few feet away, toward the wall that bordered the heath. Toby stiffened. It was probably just a squirrel. He stood surveying the area from where the sound had come. The brambles were too thick to make out what had made the noise.

It came again, the sound of something crawling through the undergrowth. It sounded bigger than a squirrel. Toby imagined Miriam Darkwater crouched among the brambles, creeping toward him.

Why would she be? He was trying to help. She had no reason to scare him.

Unnerved, he hurried back to the front drive, securing the gate with the stone again. Obviously it had just been a squirrel — or maybe a wild rabbit. As he reached the front door he heard the main gate click open and, turning, saw Albert step into view.

That was too close.

He punched in the security code and slipped inside Darkwater House, running for the stairs rather than risking a wait for the lift and an uncomfortable confrontation with his landlord.

Was it possible he'd gotten this all wrong? That Albert was innocent of killing his mother? As he took the stairs two at a time, the bag of gloves and pruning shears banging against his thigh, he began to think he had.

Chapter Twenty

"What exactly did you *not* understand about *'don't do anything stupid while I'm at work'*?" asked Sean.

They were sitting in Sean's kitchen at the breakfast bar and Toby was finding it hard to focus on what Sean was saying, as he was still wearing his work clothes, including his tool belt and those heavy brown boots. The jeans were particularly faded around the crotch, which gave the impression that Sean's cock and balls could burst through the fabric at any second.

"I really just want to give you a blow job right now," he said, hoping the offer might bring the lecture to an end.

"No sex until you tell me what the hell you were thinking of," said Sean.

"I was thinking I might be able to uncover the murder of an innocent woman," said Toby, suddenly feeling angry. "And since when did I have to ask your permission before doing something? I did get to the age of twenty-six without having you there to support me."

Sean nodded and stood to open the fridge, and as he bent to grab a beer from the bottom shelf, the material of his work jeans strained against his muscular arse. Toby envied the men who got to work alongside him and see that view all day. Although, perhaps they wouldn't appreciate it quite as much as he did.

"So, there was no body," said Sean, returning to his stool.

"Not that I could see," said Toby. "And I don't think the well was even wide enough to take a body — not even a small one."

"Then maybe we should give up," said Sean. "All we've been going on is the word of a slightly nuts woman who neither of us know — and a dream you had in the bath."

"It wasn't a dream," insisted Toby.

"Vision, then," said Sean. "It's still a long way from being firm evidence."

Toby had to admit it was.

"Maybe we should just enjoy getting to know each other for a bit, rather than acting like we're in a crime drama," said Sean.

"It would be a lot less stressful," said Toby. "But what about her — the ghost? If we don't get to the bottom of what happened, she's probably going to keep hounding me."

"It's only for a few more weeks, then you'll be gone," said Sean. "I doubt she'll follow you to your next flat."

Toby felt a wave of depression at the reality of having to find a new home and raise the money to pay for it.

"I bet you can't wait to be rid of me," said Toby.

"Hardly," said Sean. "I was in a deep depression before you came along with all your drama and hotness. Now I'm only intermittently miserable."

"I'm glad I've helped," said Toby.

"You really have," said Sean, squeezing Toby's hand.

"Does that mean I can give you that blow job now?" asked Toby, staring longingly at Sean's crotch.

"I've been working all day and I haven't had a shower," said Sean.

"Not a problem for me," replied Toby, licking his lips.

Sean laughed. "Go on then," he said. "But don't get cum all over my work jeans."

Toby slid from his stool, maintaining eye contact with Sean until he was on his knees. He pushed Sean's legs apart and nuzzled the faded crotch area, breathing in the smell of hard-earned sweat. Sean's cock began to swell, pushing against the denim. Toby kissed the growing outline, feeling its heat and pulse. He slowly unbuttoned Sean's fly, releasing more of the intoxicating aroma of sweat. His dark briefs were already stained with pre-cum, the head of Sean's cock poking above the waistband. Sean lifted his arse from the stool so that Toby could pull his jeans down a little farther. Next, he peeled the briefs back, hooking the hem under Sean's balls so that his impressive length was completely uncovered and lying flat against his T-shirt. Toby licked it from balls to head. The taste was delicious. It was the taste of a hardworking man, fresh from a day of laboring.

Toby worked with his tongue and lips, occasionally using his hand to bring Sean's orgasm closer. Sean writhed on his stool, releasing deep groans of pleasure, using his fingers to play with Toby's hair.

"I'm going to come," he said, eventually. And with a final loud groan, his cock released jet after jet of cum into Toby's waiting mouth. Toby gulped it down it as if he were drinking at a water fountain.

With a sigh of pleasure, Toby swallowed the last drop and stood, his face burning. He was rock-hard. Sean smiled, leaving his still-erect cock on display.

"Now how much more fun was that than looking for corpses?" he said.

"Much more," said Toby, savoring the after-taste of Sean's seed. "Would you bend over the stool for me? I really want to rim that hole of yours."

"You are a horny little devil this evening," said Sean, but he stood and turned around, resting his forearms on the stool and pushing his butt out toward Toby, his jeans hitched just below his thighs.

Toby nuzzled the cleft of his arse, breathing in the scent of sweat, then he parted the cheeks with his hands and began to tease the rim of Sean's tight hole with his tongue, enjoying the metallic tang and the obvious pleasure his actions were giving Sean, who groaned, pushing his butt back even farther.

Toby jabbed the point of his tongue inside Sean's hole, causing him to gasp with pleasure.

"Fuck yeah, Toby, that feels amazing."

"You taste fucking great," whispered Toby, delving his tongue in again and again, lapping at Sean's hole as it pulsed in response.

Toby buried his face between Sean's arse cheeks, taking several long, deep breaths before finally leaning back then standing.

"Now you need to take care of this for me," he said, unbuttoning his fly and pulling out his already-dripping dick.

"With pleasure," said Sean, twisting around and dropping to his knees.

Sean hadn't sucked him before and there was something incredibly erotic about being serviced by this masculine man who was still dressed for working on a building site. Toby relished the roughness of Sean's stubbled chin as he ran his tongue along Toby's shaft.

"Fuck yeah," breathed Toby, stroking Sean's head.

Sean kissed Toby's ball sack, gently sucking one testicle into his mouth and rolling it between his lips, before releasing it and returning his attention to the cockhead, teasing out a bubble of pre-cum with his tongue. He looked up at Toby as he worked, and the sight of those beautiful brown eyes staring into his brought on Toby's first wave of orgasm. He tried to control it, wanting the pleasure to go on for longer, but with a groan, he came, spattering cum against Sean's face, some running down his chin and some smearing his lips.

"Jesus," gasped Sean, obviously taken by surprise.

"Sorry," said Toby. "I didn't have time to warn you."

Sean licked his lips then scooped a glob of cum from his chin with a finger, which he slipped into his mouth. "Not a problem," he said, standing and kissing Toby on the lips. Toby tasted his own cum on Sean's mouth.

They held each other, both breathing heavily, hearts pounding, their cocks still hard and pressed together.

Sean kissed Toby twice then pushed his own cock back into his briefs, breaking the post-sex spell.

"Now I really do need to shower," he said. "I'm meeting Jess this evening, just to get back some stuff that I left at her place."

Toby was hit by a bolt of jealousy.

"Good job we don't need to search for the well after all, then," he said, hoping he didn't sound as clingy as he felt.

"Real life goes on," said Sean.

"Of course," said Toby, buttoning his fly. "Well, I'll leave you to it."

"Maybe I'll see you later," said Sean, showing Toby to the door.

"Maybe," said Toby. "Text first though, in case I get an early night."

Toby felt deflated as he returned to his flat. Not only had he wasted his day searching for a body that wasn't there, but he was left worrying that Sean might rekindle something with his ex-girlfriend, while he could still taste his cum. *How do I get into these situations?*

He thought about going to the shop for some wine. That would be the easy thing to do, just sink into a warm, drunken stupor and forget all his cares. But he decided against it. He was enjoying having some time off the booze.

He opened the fridge to see what food he had in. It looked like held be ordering a take-away, unless he fancied a moldy tomato and some week-old baked beans for dinner. He checked in the cupboard above the breakfast bar. There were two bottles of red wine standing side by side on the bottom shelf. Toby stared at them. He hadn't put them there.

Albert.

He tried to remember when he had last looked in this cupboard, shuddering at the thought of Albert creeping around his flat when he wasn't there — or even worse, while he was sleeping.

He closed the cupboard, resolved to forget that the wine was there. He'd have a shower, then order some Chinese.

* * * *

By nine o'clock that evening, feeling bloated after eating enough Chinese food for three people, Toby lay on the sofa, trying not to let his anxiety over Sean and his ex-girlfriend gnaw away at him. He hated himself for feeling like this. It was like Joe all over again. Although even with Joe, they'd been dating for a few months before the jealousy had kicked in. He and Sean hadn't made any commitment to each other. They were basically just mates who had sex, which made it even more probable that Sean would end up in bed with Jess.

Fuck it!

Toby stomped to the kitchen, flinging open the kitchen cupboard. He glared at the wine bottles as if they had said something offensive, then grabbed hold of one and searched for a clean glass.

He hated to admit it, but after the first sip, he felt more relaxed.

Eleven o'clock came and went, and Sean still hadn't come home.

So much for 'maybe see you later'.

Toby thought about opening the second bottle of wine, but his eyes were already drooping. He hauled himself from the sofa and plodded through to the bedroom, flinging himself onto the bed, still fully clothed. At least Sean had had the decency to go back to her place rather than bringing her here, where he'd have heard them giggling in the hallway.

Finally, he found the energy to undress and slip under the bed covers, but he lay awake until midnight, watching the minutes tick by, straining to hear Sean's door open and close.

He woke several times during the night, each time wondering where Sean was. Had he come home in the early hours, or was he really snuggled up with Jess in her bed? He got up at seven the next morning, too agitated to sleep in.

He wanted to find out where Sean was and if he was alone, but how did he do that without seeming needy? He had no claim on Sean. Just because the sex was incredible didn't mean it had to be exclusive. Although the thought of sleeping with anyone else had no appeal to Toby now.

He opened the front door, peering out into the corridor as if it would give a clue as to Sean's whereabouts. He'd need to leave for work in around an hour. From the end of the corridor came the sound of the lift door pinging open, then Sean appeared, jogging up the passageway. He was dressed in clean jeans and a white T-shirt that was heavily creased. He seemed flustered. When he saw Toby, he looked panic-stricken.

"Morning," said Toby. "Good night?"

"Toby, it's not what it looks like." He made to approach Toby's flat, but Toby had already closed the door. He didn't care if he seemed needy. *How could he share passion like we did then go back to his ex for a night?*

"Toby!" Sean banged on the door. "Toby, I have to get ready for work, but I'll speak to you later. You don't have to worry. I promise."

"Who's worried?" shouted Toby. "How do you know I wasn't shagging my ex last night too? It wouldn't be the first time."

Toby went through to the kitchen, closing the door behind him so that Sean's lies would at least be muffled. But Sean didn't call out again.

Toby slammed a fist into the breakfast bar and angry tears pricked his eyes.

Bastard!

His phone bleeped from the pocket of his dressing gown. He fished it out, wiping tears from his eyes so he could read the message. It was from Sean. Toby read it once to himself then out loud.

I think I know where the body is.
And I didn't sleep with Jess.

Chapter Twenty-One

"So, tell me what you meant in your text," said Toby, handing Sean a beer and sitting in one of the armchairs rather than next to Sean on the sofa.

"I didn't sleep with Jess," said Sean. "I didn't even think about it. I was only with her an hour."

"I meant the bit about the body," said Toby.

Sean nodded. "I saw Jess in a pub in Camden Town, and as I was leaving, I bumped into Lilly Darkwater. She said she lived in Camden, didn't she? Anyway, we got chatting and she asked if there was any update, so I told her about getting into the cellar but that Albert had come back early from visiting his friend in Edgware. As soon as I mentioned the friend in Edgware, you could see she was having a lightbulb moment. She said that when she was about fourteen and Albert was in his twenties, she was visiting home from boarding school and she noticed Albert kept disappearing for several hours most days and that he was always vague about where he was going. One day she followed him, hoping he was doing something he shouldn't be so that she would have something over him the next time he tried to bully her.

"To cut a long story short, he got the tube to Edgware and walked to a nice detached house on a leafy suburban road. Lilly watched from a safe distance but saw her brother ring the bell and a handsome, much older guy open the door. According to Lilly, it was obvious there was something between them. She said she could just sense an intimacy, whatever that means. A few seconds after the front door closed, she saw the older guy at the bedroom window on the first floor, drawing the curtains, and her suspicions were confirmed."

"And she thinks his current friend in Edgware is this same guy?" asked Toby.

"We went to the house last night," said Sean. "Lilly is quite an impulsive woman. She said she could still remember how to get there from the tube station. She convinced me to go with her and I just got caught up in her excitement. When we got there, she also persuaded me to go and ring the bell. I'd had a couple of pints in the pub, which gave me a bit of extra courage, so I ran to the front door, rang the bell then ran back to where Lilly was hiding behind a hedge. We could just see the front door of the house through a gap in the leaves."

"You're like a kid playing 'knock down ginger'," said Toby, shaking his head.

"Eventually the front door opened and this old guy was standing there, using a walking frame and looking like he could keel over at any second. I felt a bit bad for disturbing him. I asked Lilly if it was the guy she remembered and she said she thought it was, although it was hard to tell some thirty-odd years later."

"Then what?" asked Toby.

"I went back with Lilly to hers for a quick nightcap and to make sure she got home safely. The next thing I know, I'm waking up on her sofa with a blanket over me and it's six a.m."

"So, you spent the night with Albert's sexy younger sister," said Toby. "And I still don't get what this has got to do with knowing where Miriam's body is."

"We think it's buried in the back garden at the Edgware house," said Sean. "According to Lilly, Albert used to drive. She thinks the car may still be in the garage at the side of the house, but after his mother disappeared, he stopped using it. She never put two and two together until now, but she thinks he may have used the car to transport Miriam's body to his lover's house and buried it on the property."

"It's a bit of a stretch," said Toby.

"Oh right," said Sean, "and everything else we've come up with has been based on solid evidence. It makes sense to me. Albert has an older lover with a big garden — an older lover he thinks no one knows anything about. He doesn't even know about Lilly following him that day. She decided to keep his secret. Where better to bury the body than a garden that's barely overlooked and that no one has any reason to connect with Albert?"

"So, Albert has been seeing the same man for like forty years and never told anybody about him?" said Toby. "That's sad."

"I guess he's from a different generation than us," said Sean. "When he started seeing this guy, their relationship would actually have been illegal, remember? Albert may even have been below the age of consent when it started. Maybe that's why it started out as a secret. Then keeping it secret just became the norm. Who knows? Maybe the Edgware guy has his reasons for not wanting people to know."

"I think I know the reasons," said Toby. "In the diary we found in the cellar, Albert talks about a man called John, a Soho gangster who was married with a house somewhere in the suburbs. I think Albert's Edgware friend and John from the diary are the same man."

"So, it all ties up," said Sean.

"But how do we find out if Lilly's theory is correct?" asked Toby. "We can hardly sneak into a back garden in Edgware and start digging."

"We could if we said we were from the gas board and that we needed to investigate a problem with corroded pipes," said Sean.

"You've really thought about this, haven't you?" Toby laughed. "And since when were you the risk-taker in this partnership?"

"I might need another couple of beers to give me some Dutch courage, but I'm up for giving it a go, although I did have a nightmare last night that we got caught in the act and arrested for fraudulently gaining access to a pensioner's garden."

"I hate to be the voice of reason," said Toby, "but I don't think we should rush into this."

Secretly, Toby was annoyed that it had taken an evening with Lilly to get Sean properly excited about exposing Albert as a killer.

"I have to work the rest of the week anyway," said Sean, "but I was going to suggest Saturday—unless Albert's planning to visit him that day, in which case we'll have to reschedule."

"Okay," said Toby. "I'll get some spades from the garden center tomorrow so we're prepared. And we'll need some clothes to make us look like gas engineers. What do they even look like?"

"I can lay my hands on some overalls with reflective patches. And I have a spare pair of work boots you can borrow. You'll look hot in them."

"This is wild," remarked Toby. "Imagine if we do find the body and get Albert convicted. It will make a great feature. Plus, hopefully Miriam will stop haunting me. She's been quiet recently. She must know we're getting closer."

"Right," said Sean, standing and placing his empty beer bottle on the coffee table. "I need an early night. This moonlighting as a detective is really taking it out of me."

* * * *

If Toby hadn't made the decision to follow Albert that morning, everything could have worked out fine. But as he reached the road, having returned from a walk over the heath via the muddy track that ran alongside Darkwater House, he saw Albert just a few yards away, striding toward the main road which led to Hampstead High Street and the underground station. Of course, he could have just been going to get some shopping or popping out for a coffee in a nearby café, but Toby had a sixth sense that he was heading to visit his friend. If he was wrong, he'd have only wasted a few minutes of his time. If he was right, he might be able to get something on record of Albert acting suspiciously — a grain of evidence to show the police if Saturday's venture went awry.

Perhaps he was just feeling left out of the action — having heard second-hand about Sean and Lilly's evening together—and wanted to claim back some of the adventure for himself.

He kept a sensible distance behind Albert, who, as Toby had suspected, turned in to the underground station. Toby hovered by the entrance, waiting until Albert had negotiated the ticket barrier and stepped into a waiting lift before following. He took another lift and followed the signs for trains to Edgware. He peered along the platform and saw Albert sitting on a bench some twenty yards to his left. Toby turned right and sat between two men, one of whom was chunky and provided a good barrier between himself and Albert.

The train arrived within two minutes and Toby boarded, checking to see that Albert had too. All trains went the same way, so it was pretty much a given that he would. There was no guarantee that he would alight at Edgware, though. Maybe he had friends who lived elsewhere along the Northern Line, although Toby couldn't imagine Albert having a wide social circle.

Fifteen minutes later the trained rolled into Edgware. Toby recalled the last time he had been there and his first meeting with Albert. It was hard to believe that it had only been about five weeks before. He stepped out onto the wide central platform and saw Albert already cantering up the stairs to the exit. He moved fast for a man in his sixties. Toby had to break into a trot to keep pace.

He managed to trail Albert to a large detached house that was set on a pleasant tree-lined avenue. A short gravel driveway led down to the front door, which was painted a cheery blue. It didn't feel like a house that concealed a dark secret. Toby hung back on the opposite side of the road, partly hidden by a bushy hedge. He took out his mobile phone, pressed the camera icon and selected Record. He filmed Albert walking down the driveway. Rather than ring the doorbell, the old man continued around the side of the house. Toby sprinted across the road, paused briefly at the top of the driveway then crept down to the house, cringing at each crunching step across the gravel. He peeked around the side of the house. There was no security gate, just a narrow walkway leading to the garden. Albert had disappeared from view.

Toby walked slowly along the path, ducking under a stained-glass window. He reached the end of the side wall and saw the garden spread out before him. It was mostly lawn, well-kept, unlike the garden at Darkwater House. Albert was some fifty feet away, heading to the rear of the garden where a small copse of trees grew. There was also a shed and an old summer house, which looked in a state of disrepair. Albert stopped by the shed. He stood as if surveying the trees for a sign of something, then he dropped to his knees, his hands clasped together. Toby was still recording.

Suddenly Toby's phone burst into life, the ring tone blaring out like a siren in the near silence of the garden. Albert turned and stared directly at the spot where Toby stood. Toby leaped backward, turned and sprinted toward the road, not stopping until he had put at least three hundred yards between himself and the house. He bent over, resting his hands on his knees and taking several deep breaths.

Had Albert had time to recognize him? If so, Toby had just blown their plans.

He watched the video footage of Albert seemingly praying on the lawn. It was certainly weird behavior, but hardly enough to convince the police to reopen a ten-year-old missing persons case and dig up a sick old man's garden.

To avoid any chance of bumping into Albert at the tube station, Toby called an Uber. It was money he didn't have, but anything was preferable to being forced to explain himself to Albert.

In the taxi, he sent a text to Sean, telling him what had happened and attaching the video. He knew Sean would have a go at him for following Albert, but he might as well come clean.

Traffic was bad on the journey home. A lorry had broken down on one of the main roads and it was nearly an hour before the taxi finally drew up at Darkwater House. Toby thanked the driver with exaggerated politeness. The last time he'd used an Uber taxi, his star rating had plummeted from five to less than four, so he'd obviously done something to upset that driver.

He continued to check his phone as he punched in the security code for the outside gate, hoping for a response from Sean and also apprehensive about what that response would be. He was vaguely aware of a car pulling up behind him, the ticking of a black cab's meter and a door opening and slamming. As he pushed open the gate, someone spoke very close to his ear.

"I have a gun. Walk to the house without drawing attention to us and head straight to my flat. We need to have a little chat."

It was Albert.

Chapter Twenty-Two

Toby tested the tightness of the rope that Albert had used to bind his wrists behind the hardbacked chair. To give him credit, Albert knew how to tie a good knot. Toby's ankles were also bound. The chair was positioned in the kitchen of Albert's flat, a room Toby hadn't seen until now. It bore all the hallmarks of a once-grand, modern kitchen that had been left to go to seed — water stains on the ceiling, a white-tiled floor smeared with grease and God knew what else, cupboard doors hanging off their hinges... No wonder he hadn't invited Toby back here before.

"Why couldn't you just keep out of my business?" said Albert, nudging Toby's nose with the tip of the gun barrel. "We could have all got along nicely."

The old man smirked and stroked the gun barrel along Toby's cheek.

"I gave you every opportunity to get along with me."

Without warning, Albert prodded the gun against Toby's crotch. Toby's balls retracted, as if retreating from danger.

"You could have had a life of luxury," whispered Albert.

"Right," said Toby, trying to stop his voice from shaking. "A life of luxury doing sexual favors for an old pervert with a mummy complex, living in a decaying house."

Remember… He murdered his mother. Don't bait him, Toby's rational side boomed inside his head.

"So, what is the deal?" continued Toby. "You killed your mother because you resented having to look after her rather than getting cozy with your sugar daddy?"

"Shut up!" spat Albert, pushing the gun barrel more firmly against Toby's balls.

"I'm not judging," said Toby, hastily, suddenly very conscious that the deranged man could pull the trigger at any moment. "I totally get it. You gave up your life to look after her, when you could have been living it up in Edgware."

"My friend was married," said Albert, finally taking a few steps back and pointing the gun at the floor. "So, that wasn't an option. His wife only died a few years ago, the annoying old bitch. She was ill for decades, but she refused to die and leave him in peace. Somehow, she knew everything that went on in his life, even though she'd been in a nursing home since the early 1980s. It cost poor John a fortune, keeping her there."

"Old women really have a habit of messing with your life," said Toby.

"It wasn't just that. John, my friend, is a powerful man," said Albert. He sounded boastful, perhaps glad to have a literally captive audience with whom to finally share his secret. "When I told you I knew people who could get you out of the flat, it's through John that I know those kinds of people. He's done some terrible things in his time, back when he was younger. But he got rich off the back of them."

"You're telling me your friend in Edgware is a former gangster," said Toby, although he already knew the answer to that from reading Albert's diary.

"He was always kind to me," said Albert, looking distant. "Never aggressive. But I saw him deal with some of his, shall we say 'colleagues', when they'd messed up a job, and I had no doubt he had a vicious side. I saw him kill a man once—clubbed him over the head with a paperweight while I watched."

"Sounds lovely," said Toby.

"Oh, what would you know?" sneered Albert. "What do you know about real, passionate love? That's what John and I had. And it's still there, which I bet you find disgusting. Two old men, one in his eighties, still madly in love. Do you think you and Sean will last that long? You two won't last out the year, let alone nearly four decades. He's my world. Do you understand what that means? I wouldn't care if he was hideously disfigured by some disease. I'd still love him. I will love him until the day he dies."

Albert took a deep breath, clutching his chest. His eyes looked distant for a moment.

"Anyway," he continued, suddenly back in the room. "His being queer wouldn't have sat well with a lot of the people in his world, so we had to be discreet for that reason, too. I was always just his friend. I'm sure most of them guessed the truth, but as long as no one actually said anything, it was okay. His wife wasn't quite so understanding. She twigged pretty early on and made life as difficult as possible for us, poisoning people against us from her sick bed."

"At least your friend's wife isn't haunting you, like your mother is," said Toby.

"What?" Albert looked genuinely surprised.

"I've seen her," said Toby. "Apparently I have a talent for it. She seems very pissed off. She showed me how you killed her in the bath."

Albert staggered back another step. He almost backed into a small door set into the wall behind him, below a sloping section of ceiling. Toby guessed this was the entrance to the cellar that Lilly had mentioned.

"You keep going on about baths," he said. "You're obsessed with bloody baths."

"I know you killed her, Albert. Isn't that why we're here, with me tied to a chair and you waving a gun around? I take it that's a gift from your gangster boyfriend. She showed me how you did it, by holding her head under the bathwater."

"What do you mean she showed you?" demanded Alfred.

"Then what?" continued Toby. "You loaded her wet body into the back of your car and drove it to your friend's house in Edgware? Maybe, with his track record, it wasn't the first shallow grave he'd help dig."

"I loved my mother," said Albert, sitting in another hardbacked chair, shuffling it around until he faced Toby. The wooden legs screeched against the tile floor. "I've kept this place going for her. I found people who would feed her love of misery."

"*Her* love of misery?" Toby eyed the gun warily, but Albert seemed to have forgotten he was even holding it. It now lay in his lap, his fingers curled loosely around it.

"Oh yes," said Albert. "After my father left her, she started to fill the house with sad, needy losers like you. She basked in their unhappiness. If she was going to be miserable, then she wanted everyone around her to be."

"That's not the version I heard," said Toby, still trying to create some give in the rope around his wrists but making no headway.

"Heard from who?" demanded Albert, suddenly alert again.

"Never mind," said Toby, deciding it was a bad idea to introduce Albert's sister into the already-tense scenario. "I just understood from what you said that your mother was a caring person, that she genuinely wanted to help people. Are you sure you weren't interpreting her kindness through your own warped mind? Maybe the people she rented to were unhappy at first, but she was trying to help them, wasn't she?"

Albert laughed humorlessly.

"If you say so," he said.

"You tell me," said Toby. "I'm genuinely interested to hear your side of the story."

"I have told you," snapped Albert, waving the gun like an extension of his hand. "She was a bitter, twisted old woman who created an environment of misery. And I was trapped in it with her for years, because she couldn't bear the thought of me leaving her the way my father had. You say you've seen her. Does she seem like a benevolent woman to you?"

Toby pictured the tortured, ravaged face.

"Not exactly," he admitted.

"Everything I do is for her."

"Out of guilt?" asked Toby.

Albert didn't respond.

"You killed her to be free, then carried on living the exact same life," continued Toby.

"Ironic, isn't it," said Albert. "I've become my mother — a sad old loner, surrounded by even sadder losers."

"Would she have gone out of her way to try to stop two people from being together, the way you have with Sean and me?" asked Toby.

"Of course she would," said Albert. "That's exactly the kind of thing she would have done."

Toby remembered the hideous vision of Albert's dead mother standing in the hallway outside his flat. He had been trying to get to Sean, but some force — presumably Miriam Darkwater's ghost — had held the door closed. Maybe Albert wasn't lying about his mother's bitter nature. Just because she wanted revenge on her murderous son might not mean she wasn't also happy to try to disrupt a blossoming relationship at the same time.

Bloody cheek! Using us to expose Albert while trying to end our romance, thought Toby.

"My mother embodied anger and resentment," said Albert. "I couldn't stand any more of it. So, yes, I killed her. But as soon as I'd done it, I felt racked with guilt and mortified by what I'd done. I did love her. So, being stuck here, surrounded by misery, is my penance, if you like. My homage to her memory."

"And what about when you kill me?" asked Toby, "Will you feel guilty then? Did you feel guilty after you helped drive poor Susan to suicide?"

"That was never the plan," said Albert, actually looking ashamed.

"And me?" asked Toby. "Are you actually planning to kill me? Would you seriously be able to put a bullet in my head while I stare straight into your eyes?"

Albert hesitated. He glanced down at the gun, examining it like a toy he had just unwrapped, then met Toby's gaze.

"What choice do I have?" he asked. "You know what I did, don't you? I need to protect John, if nothing else. He's too old and ill to face charges. He was just helping me. I couldn't live with myself if the strain of all this killed him."

"You really think you could do it?" asked Toby. "And what about Sean? Will you shoot him too? He knows everything I know. He may have been to the police already. And what about when people come asking after us? Will you kill them too? I mean, I know I don't exactly have a great circle of friends, but there are people who would eventually notice I was gone. I have parents, for a start, who know I'm living here now. Are you going to shoot my mother in the head too? I guess you wouldn't find that hard. If you can murder your own mother, I suppose killing someone else's would be easy."

"Stop going on," said Albert. "You're making my head hurt."

Toby saw something move in the kitchen doorway. He glanced in that direction and gasped. She was there, her black dress billowing around her as if caught in a draft, and her face was a mask of hatred. She was staring at Albert, her eyes blazing, mouth gaping.

"What is it?" demanded Albert, looking toward the doorway and back to Toby.

"She's here," said Toby. "And she looks really annoyed. I think she's finally going to get her revenge on you, Albert."

"Don't lie," said Albert, but he kept staring at the doorway. As he stared, Miriam pointed directly at him, her arm stripped of flesh like the branch of a silver birch tree.

"She's pointing at you," said Toby, enjoying his captor's discomfort but also terrified by the appearance of Miriam's ghost.

Miriam glided across the kitchen until she stood behind Albert's chair. The stray strands of hair on Albert's pale scalp stirred and stood upright. He patted his head with the hand that wasn't holding the gun, and looked behind him, obviously sensing his mother's presence.

"What is she doing now?" he asked, his voice rising in pitch.

Miriam lifted a hand to her temple as if to salute, but at the last second formed the two-finger representation of a gun.

"I think she's suggesting you kill yourself," said Toby.

"No!" Albert leaped to his feet, and his mother's ghost rose toward the ceiling so that she looked down at him, fingers still resting against her head. "Mother!"

"I don't think she feels very maternal right now," said Toby.

"She loved me!" shrieked Albert, turning in circles, his gun hand flailing dangerously.

"That was before you ducked her head under the bath water and killed her," said Toby.

"I'm sorry. Mother!" screamed Albert. "Please let me see you. I want to tell you to your face how sorry I am. I wanted to kill myself after what I did. It was John who stopped me, made me believe it was worth going on."

Toby watched as Miriam continued to tap two fingers against her temple.

"She isn't softening," he told Albert. "She says you should shoot yourself in the head."

The old man turned on him, pointing the gun with a quivering hand.

"Fuck you!" he screamed, and Toby closed his eyes, waiting for the blast, his insides clenched like a fist.

He heard a click, a thud then the sound of something shattering. When he opened his eyes, Albert was lying face down on the floor, his head bleeding and surrounded by fragments of what looked like shells and china. Standing over him, holding the base of what Toby assumed had been the hideous shell lamp from the cellar, was Sean. Behind him, the door to the cellar was open.

"Hi," said Toby, lamely. "I'm really sorry about this."

Sean ran to him, dropping to his knees to unfasten his ankles then working on the ropes around his wrists.

"Are you okay?" he asked.

"Yeah, I'm fine," Toby reassured him, glancing around the kitchen for a sign of Miriam, but she had gone. "How did you know I was here?"

"I came back to the house when I got your text. I was waiting in my flat and I saw Albert marching you down the front drive. I managed to get back down to the cellar in the lift, but the lights weren't working. Lilly told me where I could find a key to the door into the kitchen, but it took me ages to find it in the dark. Lilly is on her way with the police, by the way...or she should be. Maybe she's having trouble explaining everything."

Hands finally free, Toby pulled Sean toward him, wrapping his arms around the other man's broad shoulders and kissing him on the mouth.

"Thanks," said Toby, as they broke their embrace. "This officially makes you my hero."

Chapter Twenty-Three

Toby woke at the touch of Sean's lips against his. He squinted up into his lover's face. Bright sunshine was streaming into the room. It took Toby a moment to remember which room he was in, not because he was hungover, but because he and Sean alternated whose flat they stayed in and because they saw each other so often that he sometimes forgot which bed he'd finally gone to sleep in.

The night before, he and Sean had had a quick drink at one of the many local pubs then watched a movie at the Everyman Cinema before heading back to Sean's for several hours of wonderful sex.

"Are you planning to get up at all today?" asked Sean, placing a mug of coffee on the bedside table. "We're meant to be going for a walk. It'll be dark by the time you stir your bones."

"What time is it?" asked Toby.

"Half eight," said Sean.

"That's not late!" protested Toby. "It's Saturday. I normally lie in until ten...sometimes eleven."

"Not now that you're my boyfriend," said Sean, kissing him again. "See you in the kitchen in ten minutes for breakfast."

Toby watched Sean walk away, still so turned on by his perfect arse, currently clad in a pair of tight black briefs. He took a deep breath and stretched as he sat up. It had been five weeks since Albert had been arrested and carted off by the police. His trial wouldn't be for several months, but he was in custody. His mother's body had been found in the back garden in Edgware. Albert's 'friend' had also been arrested, but he had gone downhill, health-wise, at a rapid rate and was now in a hospice rather than a prison cell.

It had certainly been an eventful few weeks. Since the day Albert had held Toby at gunpoint, things had settled down to a more sedate pace — although far from dull. Sean had become increasingly affectionate, and started talking as if they were a couple, not just two friends who enjoyed having sex. They went on proper dates and had even talked about going away for a long weekend.

Since Albert's removal, life at Darkwater House had taken a more pleasant turn for everyone who lived there. It was as if someone had opened all the windows and let out the bad atmosphere created by Albert — and, if he were to be believed, his mother before him. The tenants spoke to each other now, and meetings in the lift or the communal hallway seemed to be more commonplace, as if the house was pushing them together. The couple who had always seemed to be rowing could often be seen walking hand-in-hand along the front drive, and Derrick, the guy who always seemed to have a book in his hand, was often paying a visit to flat three, where the young woman lived who had thrown up at the sight of poor Susan's body. Gita, the nurse, was convinced there was a romance blooming between them. She said she could often hear them giggling together in Derrick's flat, and once she was pretty certain she heard them having sex. Toby pictured Gita with her ear pressed to a wall, straining to hear events unfold in her neighbor's apartment.

Toby finished his coffee and wandered through to the kitchen. He was taken aback to find Gita sitting at the breakfast bar with Sean, who seemed quite happy to parade in front of her wearing just a T-shirt and underpants. Toby was glad he'd bothered to pull on a dressing gown. Gita was prone to get a little too touchy-feely, especially if she'd had a drink. And because she worked such unsociable hours, he never knew when she might have downed a glass of wine.

'It's evening for me,' she'd said when Toby had commented on her tipsy state at ten o'clock one Tuesday morning. *'I worked all night.'*

"Morning," said Gita. "I just popped in to tell you guys the good news."

She sounds sober.

"What good news?" asked Toby, pouring himself another coffee from the cafetière.

"Lilly, Albert's sister, is moving in to his old flat and taking over as landlady. I just saw her in the hallway. Apparently, the house has always been half hers. She just stayed away because of her nutty brother. She seems nice."

"Yeah," said Toby. "We saw Lilly a couple of weeks ago and she told us that was the plan."

"Would you like another coffee, Gita?" asked Sean, nodding at her empty mug.

"No, I'd better head off to bed," said Gita. "Maybe see you for a drink later? I'm not working until Sunday night."

"We're having a quiet night in," said Toby, showing her to the door.

Gita's face fell.

"But you're welcome to join us if you want," he relented. "We'll just have a few beers and watch a movie. You can bring snacks. Maybe we'll ask Lilly too."

"Oh, cool!" enthused Gita. "I'd love that. See you later."

Sean was smiling when Toby returned to the kitchen. "You're not such a bad lad really," he said.

"I'm a bloody martyr," said Toby, but he smiled too. "I'll have a shower and we can get out for that walk before it starts raining."

* * * *

Lilly was standing in the communal hallway, barking commands at two burly men who were carrying a bulky three-seater sofa between them. It wouldn't fit in with Albert's inherited sixties chic, Toby considered, but maybe that was the idea.

"Oh, hi, boys!" she greeted as they stepped out of the lift. "I've finally got some of my furniture out of storage. I'm assuming Albert won't be back any time soon."

"The evidence is rather stacked against him," agreed Toby.

"Psycho," added Sean.

"Now, now," said Lilly, casting a chastising look in Sean's direction. "He's not well. You have to feel sorry for him, really."

"He held me at gunpoint," Toby reminded her.

"And he drowned your mother," said Sean.

"Yes, point taken," said Lilly. "Do you both want to join me for a drink later?"

"No, come and join us," said Toby. "We already have the lovely Gita popping by."

"I was going to suggest a little gathering at mine," said Lilly, scowling at the two men as they struggled to get the sofa through the front door of her flat. "I've already invited the couple from the first floor and the boy that lives next to them…"

"I don't think we've even met him," said Sean.

"What does he look like?" asked Toby.

"Short and chubby with really bad skin," said Lilly. "Nice enough, though. I'll knock on the other doors a bit later, when these clowns have finished moving my stuff in. I'd better go before they wreck the place."

"See you later," called Sean as Lilly ran to direct the men, who were still having trouble negotiating the sofa into her flat.

* * * *

They had just reached the duck pond and were considering which route to take next when Toby saw a familiar face. Sitting on a bench, next to someone wearing a hoodie that shrouded his features from view, was Joe.

"Shit," said Toby, "that's my ex."

Sean followed Toby's gaze. "Did you want to go say hello?" he asked. "I can wait here."

"I don't know," said Toby, but as he hesitated, Joe glanced over and waved.

"Go on," said Sean. "You're in a good place. Now's the perfect time to bump into him."

Toby took a deep breath and walked over to the bench. Joe stood and opened his arms for a hug. Toby held out a hand instead, and after a confused pause, Joe shook it.

"What brings you here?" asked Toby.

"Just fancied a nice walk," said Joe.

"You're a long way from Wimbledon."

Joe coughed. "I don't live in Wimbledon anymore. Mike and I split up and I decided to be the bigger man and move out. It's a funny thing, actually. I'm living in your old flat in Islington."

"What?" Toby really hadn't seen that coming.

"Yeah," laughed Joe, although he seemed embarrassed. "When I left Mike's place — I mean, the place we shared — I came to see you. I thought maybe I could crash at yours for a bit."

"Really?" exclaimed Toby. "Out of all your friends in London, you thought *I* was the best bet?"

Joe looked even more awkward. "Most of my friends didn't get on with Mike and I told them where to go — *'Take me, take my boyfriend'* — that sort of thing. So I was a bit hard-pressed to find anyone that would take me in."

"So I was a last resort," said Toby. "Sad, desperate Toby. I bet you thought I'd be so happy to see you that I'd invite you in with open arms."

"Don't be like that," said Joe. "I always thought of you as a friend, no matter what had gone on between us. Anyway, you weren't there, obviously, but your flat was still up for rent, so I managed to sweet talk your old landlord into letting me have it without paying a deposit. He's such an old queen that he was putty in my hands. I knew he'd always fancied me."

Toby could barely remember what his former landlord had been like, just that he lived on the first floor and chain-smoked.

"Well, I hope it all works out for you," said Toby.

"Oh, it has," said Joe. "Not only do I have a new flat, but I have a new boyfriend too. You must know Luke."

"Hey, bro." The seated figure in the hoodie looked up and Toby stared in disbelief into the blue eyes of his former neighbor. The smell of stale dope wafted up as he shifted his position. "Your ex wasn't as shy as you about giving head. He gives it really good…even better than my ex-girlfriend. I suck his cock too. Turns out it tastes okay."

An elderly couple passing close to the bench cast disproving stares in their direction.

"Seriously," said Toby, "you're dating a teenage stoner?"

"Hey," objected Luke, "I turned twenty last week."

"Come on, Toby," said Joe, adopting a once-familiar patronizing expression. "No need to be like that. Surely you're not still jealous of what I get up to."

Toby threw back his head and let out a hearty laugh.

"Joe," he said, "I can honestly say that I have never felt less jealous in my life."

He considered filling Joe in on his current accommodation and pointing out Sean, who was loitering some way off, looking particularly gorgeous in a short black raincoat, faded jeans and walking boots. But he didn't feel the need to rub Joe's nose in his good fortune.

"Take care, both of you," he said, then headed back to join Sean.

"Let's go to the top of Kite Hill," he said, placing a hand on Sean's back. "I'm in the mood for that view."

* * * *

"It is a great view," said Sean, as they stood on top of Kite Hill, gazing at the London skyline. It was a beautiful, clear late autumn day, so every building stood in crisp focus. It would have made a great postcard.

"I can't believe we get to live so close to all this," said Toby.

"And we now have a sexy older woman as our landlady," said Sean. "Definitely an improvement on her creepy brother, may he rot in prison."

"I knew you fancied her," said Toby, smiling.

"I only have eyes for you, my love," replied Sean, also grinning.

"I wonder how long he'll get?" said Toby.

"I don't imagine he'll ever come out," said Sean. "I bloody hope not, anyway. Maybe he'll be declared too mad to stand trial and get off somehow. We'll wake up one night to find him crawling around the bedroom, sniffing our dirty underwear where we've thrown it on the floor."

"Don't!" laughed Toby.

"Have you seen *her* at all recently, by the way?" asked Sean.

"Miriam?" asked Toby, glancing sideways at his lover, who nodded. "No, not since her funeral. I think she's resting now that she's not in a shallow grave in Edgware."

"A shallow grave in Edgware..." mused Sean. "That would make a good book title."

"Already started it," laughed Toby. "I'm going to make us a fortune."

Sean placed a hand on Toby's back. "I like the way you just referred to 'us'," he said.

"As far as I'm concerned, there's an 'us'," said Toby, "but I don't want to put pressure on you."

"My parents are in London next week," said Sean. "I'm going to tell them about you then. I don't know why I've been so worried. They're lovely people. They teach secondary school kids and preach about acceptance all day every day. Why would they reject me for fancying another guy?"

"I'm sure they won't," said Toby. "I'd love to meet them some time, when you think they're ready."

"By the time I've finished singing your praises, they'll be begging to meet you," said Sean with a wink.

"Shall we get a beer?" asked Toby.

"Sounds like a plan," said Sean, and as they turned to head down the hill, Sean took his hand and held it tightly. He was still holding it when they reached the pub.

Want to see more from this author? Here's a taster for you to enjoy!

Mirror Man
Samuel King

Excerpt

Alfie had always dreamed of living in a house set in its own woods. In his fantasies, the house would have a tower and the woods would be expansive, sweeping down a hillside to a small village where he would buy organic vegetables from a little independent shop. But sometimes dreams required compromise, and walking through the densely packed silver birch trees toward the third house on their agenda that day, he thought this could just be that time.

"I really like it," he whispered to Tom, who strode purposefully beside him, eyeing Ashley, the enthusiastic estate agent who was a few paces ahead of them. Alfie followed Tom's gaze. It seemed to be focusing on Ashley's arse. Alfie could see the appeal of the small but perfectly formed butt, attractively presented in blue suit trousers, but he wished that, today of all days, Tom could resist temptation. This was supposed to be their new start, after all.

Ashley was fumbling with a set of keys, great clunking things hanging from a solid metal ring. Alfie loved that these were the keys to their new home — their possible new home.

"You haven't even seen it yet," said Tom.

"I've seen the pictures," Alfie replied, cold from an earlier downpour of rain but still flushed with excitement.

"Not the same," said Tom.

"Look! It's beautiful." Alfie nodded to the cottage, which had sprung into view as they'd crested the shallow slope of the mulchy pathway that wound through the copse of trees.

Ashley turned, boyish face beaming, his own neatly cut dark hair shining with rain. "It is special, isn't it?" he said.

Tom flashed Alfie a warning glance that said, *Don't let an estate agent know you like a house before you've even been inside. He'll use it against us!*

Alfie didn't care. He grinned as they approached the Victorian cottage, which had an entrance that was like something from a chapel — red bricks formed an archway, topped by a winged gargoyle that pointed a tiny clawed finger at them as they neared the front door. Perfect.

"Have we just walked into a Hammer horror film?" asked Tom, not bothering to whisper now.

"Wouldn't that be great?" laughed Alfie, quickening his pace so that he was standing next to Ashley as the agent tried the first of five keys in the lock to the front door.

The lock finally clicked and the heavy wooden door swung inward.

"Oh," said Alfie, disappointed. "No sinister creak."

"Well, you can't have everything," said Tom, giving Alfie's back an affectionate rub. Alfie stepped forward, probably leaving Tom's hand suspended.

"So, this is the entrance hall," chirped Ashley.

"Really?" said Tom. "An entrance hall inside the front door. What other surprises do you have for us, Ash?"

Tom gave Ashley's shoulder a friendly squeeze. The estate agent blushed.

It was hardly a hall, just a square space with well-trodden tiles on the floor. Wooden panels enclosed the area, with doors to their left and right and a row of coat hooks fixed to the wall that faced them. Alfie reached out and fondled one of the hooks as if it were something phallic.

"For Christ's sake," muttered Tom.

Ashley coughed. "Shall we go left or right?" he asked.

Alfie bit his lower lip, looking at each closed door in turn. "Left," he said, already grabbing the lever handle and pushing down.

The door opened onto a living room that was dominated by a huge chimney breast and a fireplace almost big enough to sit in. Above the brick mantelpiece hung an ostentatious gold-framed mirror, the glass liver-spotted and murky.

Alfie went straight to it. As he inspected the ancient piece, he caught sight of Tom's cynical expression in the reflection, distorted by grime and the fifteen or so feet from mirror to door, but still clearly scornful. It was a look that suited his hard, slightly crooked features. His wide, full-lipped mouth had been made to sneer. Alfie studied his own reflection for a moment too, noticing the fine lines around his gray eyes. He looked older than twenty-six, he thought. He was sure those lines hadn't been there six months ago, before he'd caught Tom in bed with another man. That was not the first person he'd cheated on Alfie with, he'd come to learn.

"Is this staying?" asked Alfie, nodding at the mirror.

"It can, I'm sure," said Ashley, who had moved to the French windows that offered a view across the rear garden. "In fact, yes, I'm sure it can. All the furniture comes with the house."

"Oh good," said Alfie, now bending to peer up the chimney. "Does this work?" His voice echoed, as did the laugh that followed. He knew he was being too keen and over-excited, but it wasn't as if they were planning to buy the place. They were only renting for a year — assuming their relationship lasted that long. Alfie wasn't sure that even a new start in his dream home in Devon would be enough to salvage things, but he was willing to give it a go. When he straightened up, he eyed Tom's reflection again. His boyfriend's gaze was fixed on Ashley's butt once more.

The remainder of the viewing continued to feed Alfie's glee — more wood paneling, exposed beams in every bedroom, a bathtub on clawed feet and a spiral staircase leading to a spacious attic, which was dripping in spider webs.

Alfie heard Tom and Ashley descend the spiral staircase while he continued to survey the attic. It would be the perfect workspace. *Where better than a dusty attic room to write blogs and features about horror films?*

"No!"

It was Ashley's voice, and he sounded both shocked and upset. Alfie clattered down the spiral stairs to the landing. Ashley and Tom were standing several feet apart, and the young estate agent was red with what could have been embarrassment or anger. Tom was holding up both his hands in front of him, as if to calm a spooked animal.

"What's going on?" asked Alfie, although he already knew. They hadn't even moved into the house and Tom was already up to his old tricks.

"Are you okay?" he asked Ashley.

"Yeah." The estate agent straightened his tie and headed toward the stairs. "I'll be outside if you need anything."

Alfie turned to face Tom, who had the cheek to meet his gaze without shame.

"Really, Tom? The estate agent? He's about twenty. He's not even gay. He lives with his girlfriend."

"I didn't do anything!" insisted Tom. "I just accidently brushed my hand against his arse. He's overreacting."

"Come on, Tom," said Alfie. "Let's not do this. I let you treat me like an idiot before, but I'm not going to make a habit of it. You obviously don't want to be with me, so why are we pretending you do? I love this house. Let this be my new start. You can have a new start somewhere else with whomever you want."

"Alfie..." Tom made to grab hold of his hand, but Alfie snatched it away.

"I'll see you outside," said Alfie. "I'm going to take one last look around before I tell Ashley that I want the house—assuming you haven't frightened him away."

PUBLISHING

Sign up for our newsletter and find out about all our romance book releases, eBook sales and promotions, sneak peeks and FREE romance books!

About the Author

Samuel King is London born and bred, and spent his twenties and thirties hanging out on the London gay scene, mixing with some true characters and even finding romance on a few occasions. Now more likely to be found eating in a nice restaurant on a Saturday night than clubbing, he also enjoys reading across many genres, watching films—especially old horror films and romantic comedies.

Samuel loves to hear from readers. You can find his contact information, website details and author profile page at https://www.pride-publishing.com